T0065580

DESTINED TO
LOVE

DESTINED TO LOVE

MRIDU G.

PARTRIDGE

To order additional copies of this book, contact
Partridge India
000 800 10062 62
orders.india@partridgepublishing.com

www.partridgepublishing.com/india

Dedicated to....

This book is dedicated to *life. Life,* with all its highs and lows, its misery and joys and its straight and crooked ways. *Life*, which has always righted itself just in time for another wild ride to happen.

A work in progress it is – this Book and this Life.

Many Thanks To....

This book owes gratitude to many a souls. I need to thank almost everybody who came into my life.

... Some for extremely short periods of time and some for considerable amounts of time.

... The ones who brought darkness and the ones who brought light.

... Some who came into the picture only for the book to take shape and some only when the book had taken shape.

Special thanks to Abhishek Sharma for helping with the creative and Mohit Pawar for the strong courage booster I needed to put thought to paper.

This book, Destined To Love, is the teaser for 'The Journey to Nowhere', a book about evolution and the human journey to the place where the soul will eventually find its peace. Nowhere? Or right here?

The scientific man does not aim at an immediate result. He does not expect that his advanced ideas will be readily taken up. His work is like that of the planter – for the future. His duty is to lay the foundation for those who are to come, and point the way.

—Nikola Tesla

Niti and Salil's love story forms the backdrop for a reflection on the Science of the Soul. It reinforces the fact that love is the answer to every question today – not compulsive, expected-by-society love but love that keeps the heart true and real and naturally free of dis-ease and other modern-day demons.

The study of this science is equivalent to a seven-year-old reciting multiplication tables. The children are not aware of the importance of the tables; they have yet not heard the word 'multiplication' and 'division', but they learn the tables because they are asked to. They cannot see the larger picture and have no idea that someday they could become space scientists just because they learned multiplication rules at the age of seven. Similarly, the state of society and mankind today, the turmoil we're going through, is a result of not being able to see the bigger picture. We have no idea where evolution is heading or what, out of what we're doing, is relevant and what is not. If we could see where evolution was heading, we could choose the relevant attributes to pursue – which would be soul-centric.

This is not a 'spiritual' book in the sense of the modern-day interpretation of the word 'spiritual'. It does not prescribe a path to be followed or a destination to be achieved.

No, this is a scientific book – the only difference being that one needn't be a student of science or a PhD or even scientifically minded to understand the Science of the Soul.

This is a knowledge that we all carry within us. We all relate to it, some more than others. All it requires is a little focus and contemplation of the facts. While the facts are scientific enough to require prior knowledge, the gist is universal.

You may believe that you don't have the time or the inclination at this point of time in your life to indulge in these thoughts or live out life by this science, but the fact is, if you have come upon this book, it *is* your time. Whenever you start – it is your time. Just get started. You've been doing it unconsciously forever; now is the time to do it consciously with complete understanding and in a chosen direction.

This science is personal. It's an intimate, individual growth, independent of time and structure. It is different for every person, as different *as* every person, in fact.

The Science of the Soul is a scientific process, and it has its laws and rules. Beyond that, it is your relationship with your Source.

I am not a guru, guide, master, healer or a lifestyle expert. I am not of exceptional intelligence either. I have never been an academic topper or an ace performer in any field. I was not born 'different' or gifted nor have I ever felt I was meant for bigger things. I am ordinary. My intelligence is probably average. But I have given time, deep concentration and doggedness to the study, and I believe, if I am able to understand and mould myself to the understanding, it should be possible for most others to do so too.

Even though Yukteshwar Giriji said in 1894 that it would be many centuries before man would be able to totally grasp this knowledge, I'm tempted to start discussing it now. There will be many who will be able to grasp it now as well . . .

Chapter 1

Skolt walked back towards the big, wide glass window on the right and looked out at the city below. The gentle landscape with the lights from houses that dotted the huge green expanse were usually enough to captivate him for hours. Today, though, he wasn't really seeing anything. His mind was anywhere but at the scenery stretched out before him. He turned to walk away again and abruptly stopped mid-stride, catching his wandering thoughts and consciously slowing down his rapidly moving mind-picture. What was he doing? Why was he behaving like he was actually *in* the twenty-first century – all agitated and unsure? 'Goodness! Where did that come from I wonder!' he muttered to himself, self-mockingly.

Of course, he knew where that had come from! He just didn't believe that *he* could be susceptible to memories. He – who taught the youth to reflect on their past lives dispassionately and learn how to make sense of them – was falling prey to a mind-ploy! His position as Memory Guard and Guide to the current civilisation had kind of made him immune to memory games. He never indulged in the 'Do you remember when . . .' games. Never! He was a research scientist – and far more boring than he really needed to be, truth be said. That's right. Boring. Not a hand-wringing, restless, unsure klutz. Boring.

Wouldn't Lara just love to know that he was capable of it, though? he thought wryly. Not boring – that she already knew – but the anxious, restless, and so forth, bit.

Stop.

Focus, Skolt.

The people of today could easily access their past and view it anytime they liked, even though they never seemed inclined to do so. He wondered how they could not! 'If only they knew what ignoring history had done to the world in the past!' he always thought.

But today, he wondered if it wasn't better that way. The past had a way of holding on to you. Latching on and not letting go. And he had been going back and forth with his memories for a number of days now. Most of the times he'd snap out of a thought process and feel totally confused and disoriented. He had to stop. He knew he had to. He was churning up the ether waves around him, and it would just make it that much more difficult for his team to connect with his train of thought. He needed to be completely in sync with his team at the moment. He knew how strong his thought waves were.

But the restless reflection on the past just wouldn't go.

No, this wasn't an obsession. His, Skolt's, reflection on the twenty-first century stemmed from having just commissioned a written documentation on the 'The Book of Intelligence' by his team of researchers. They were expected to search the Akashic Records and collect data from the last 40,000 to 48,000 years and compile the study. He knew intelligence being an outdated topic of discussion these days would require much effort to surface from the records.

He had only intended to bring the thoughts from his two lifetimes, both as women incidentally – one in the twentieth century of ADY and the other in the ninth century of DKY – to the fore. He knew that would bring the topic into a closer ether wave and from there it would be easier for the young scholars to go further back into what was then called 'BCE'. It was a difficult topic for them to work on, and he wondered if he wasn't being too harsh on the young guns. After all, the concepts of 'morals', 'God', 'religion', 'ego', 'surgery', and so forth, were not easy for the modern generation to grasp. These were alien thoughts in the current century of year 14016. Though 'war' and 'money' as evils of the past were taught to the youth as topics of discussion, he didn't think the new generation had ever really connected with these issues. These words were merely academic and good for debates!

He laughed humourlessly, under his breath, remembering his lifetime in the twentieth-century CE when all these concepts had been alive and relevant, and it had felt like mankind would never have a life without the struggle of war and money and sex and power.

Yes. The twentieth century. That lifetime as Niti. That era of struggle and heartache. It had been a time of huge change and turmoil – for the energies of the planet at large and, in more immediate focus, for the energies of the younger soul he had been then.

And no, his life in the twentieth-century CE had not been the hardest of his past lives. The one previous to that had been far harder, for sure. It had then involved physical as well as mental torments of unparalleled heights. But his life as Niti . . . that had wrenched his heart out of his body. Well – her body. Not literally, of course! But almost literally . . . Oh! It had been hard. Let's leave it at that.

It was just – well – he wore her well. He related to that pain the most out of all the memories of emotions he had – whenever he allowed himself to have them, that is. She had taught him to feel. To love. Totally and completely. Even whilst living in an unloved and broken state of heart.

'But that was then, and this was now,' he reminded himself. Now he didn't need, nor did he want that kind of connection. He had a purpose to fulfil. Why then were these memories niggling him? He had lived them dispassionately many a times, every time that he had looked at them in fact. He also accepted that the incomplete story of that lifetime had a purely scientific purpose in his growth. Why then was it troubling him so?

As Skolt looked out at the outline of the city below him, he thought about the images of the supposedly imaginary city called Atlantis that people had debated over for centuries, long before they had access to the Akashic Records. His city of Melita looked exactly like those pictures. In fact, he had taken images of the Atlantis and created his blueprint. He could see the twinkling lights of Melita in the distance.

Looking out at the scenery calmed him, and a little of the anguish seemed to subside. He would love to meet the soulmate he had yearned for as a woman that long lifetime ago, if only to understand why he still felt this anguish.

But . . . how?

And his mind flashed an image of 'Google'. He smiled. Yes. The search engine of the physical generation! That was what used to be used in those days. The Internet had been a wondrous discovery and totally in keeping with the bigger picture of the universe. Google was long gone, though.

That being a physical *yuga*, everything in the span of approximately 2,400 years around the twenty-first-century CE was associated with the material world or the physical world. And as we all know, the physical world had limitations. And though there was a lot of knowledge then and a lot was known and a lot was fed into the Internet and a lot was accessed, one could only access what had been put in. And one could only access from a physical machine that had been synced with the knowledge fed in, which had been converted into the written word because only language-in-form could be understood then. And for very many years it was sufficient. Google and the Internet in general used the 'cloud' concept, which was the reason it remained relevant in the universe. The information on 'cloud' just naturally became accessible through the ether, which is where the universe stores its information.

And when man went beyond the physical, he began to access knowledge directly from the ether through his senses and into his mind as language-in-impulse, rather than from the 'cloud' through the physical computer with his physical body. As the ether had all knowledge, everything ever said or done was recorded in the ether, including everything that Google had saved, dating back to—well, whenever! Anything and everything in this world could be accessed by concentrating on the knowledge required and allowing your senses to 'read' it from the ether. These are the Akashic Records, and the process of reading them is known as *sheetla*. To access personal information, one's aura or personal energy is used. This personal energy is as unique as fingerprints and with the high frequency of energy activated by humans today (14016) accessing their personal history required nothing more than thinking about it. But information about another's history was impossible to get. Energy could not be hacked, and the

Akashic Records would only read energy. So if one's energy structure did not match the information being accessed, it would be denied. For other generic information, one had to produce a concurrent level of energy, and some concepts were easily accessed, while others needed effort. Concepts such as sciences of metals, elements, human body, electricity, magnetism, crystals had been well studied and were easily accessible. The science and research of the current times was only about space and human consciousness as related to higher energies and the universe. Human connections with the surroundings was done and dusted, and human connections with the beyond were sought. The only science studied today was Science of the Soul.

Knowledge is for everyone – that is the basis of life today in 14016. It is free and available and for you to use to grow in your life. There is no test of knowledge that one has; there is no need to learn or retain any knowledge. It is a tool to be used as and when and for whatever one chooses to use it. Intelligence, therefore, is not a concept today. It is not measured or graded. One is not given personal importance or work or power based on their intelligence as it was once done. In fact, one is not *given* anything in today's world! Everything that is, is everybody's. You don't owe anyone for the land you live on or the water you drink or the air you breathe. He knew how strange that would have sounded in Niti's era.

With a little more humour in his laugh, he reflected on how in the late twentieth century and through the twenty-first-century CE stories were written about the future, and it was assumed that humans would be more machine-like and robotic, with emotions and humanness fading away gradually. He could almost see those sci-fi movies, as they were called then, in his mind's eye. He laughed out loud at the images of metallic-garment-clad people eating little capsules for meals and talking as if through a machine flashed before him. Loveless and mechanical they had thought mankind would become? If only they could have seen into the future! They would have been amazed to see how the oneness of humanity was all that sustained life in the future. And how humans had gone within themselves to live in true humanness with no support of machines or medicines or money – the three M's as they were called!

Or maybe they were better off not to have seen it – they would have been so disappointed! 'Not enough drama in the future', they'd have said!

No robotic, metallic clothes, sorry! People wore ordinary, natural cloth. Nothing synthetic was available or used. People ate food just like always – only difference being they ate when the body demanded, what the body demanded, and how the body demanded food. As to say, people are perfectly in-tune with their bodies, and they do whatever is required to keep the structure healthy. No programmed health but only natural health. And no capsules either, thankfully!

And yes, after almost killing each other and the ecosystem, man gave up the need for power through money and war in the twenty-third century. The barter system – the original way of life – thrived in the world today, and humans shared their lives freely with each other. They ate natural, lived natural, and wore natural – natural being whatever could be grown, absorbed, or retrieved from nature in their immediate surroundings. People healed themselves as they lived in perfect harmony with nature, and like all other animals in their natural habitat, man died of circumstances that arose; it was no longer considered destiny or 'God's fault or luck or any of the other helpless reasons!

In fact, what had been considered sophisticated medical ways and highly evolved methods of health correction in the ancient past were today's horror stories. People sat around the dining table and shuddered at the thought of making a human being unconscious. Taking away from a person the control of their senses and making them immobile? Ridiculous! And then invading their private energy space to cut open the physical body and remove or repair parts or even inject foreign bodies? Incredulous! How did people even allow that! 'Was there no one with even a modicum of knowledge then?' they asked in horror.

Indulgently, Skolt allowed the memory wave to move on. These medical geniuses, known as doctors, had been the highest in the barter trade supremacy – or income bracket, as it was known then. They had been next to God.

'God'! And what a big issue *that* had been in the past centuries! It had almost destroyed the planet! Well, not the recent past centuries. For the last 7,000 years people had been well aware of the true nature of existence as was required for their growth. They had stopped routing their survival via an imaginary 'God' or gods in some cases. But yes, way back – 10,000–15,000 years ago – mankind routed their everyday activities through a concept of 'God' and the 'religion' He prescribed! Before everything they did, they asked for His help, and after, they'd thank Him. They celebrated Him and cursed Him. They believed He did all that happened to life and the planet and the very universe. People had no faith in themselves – they had to create faith! But they had huge amounts of faith in the imaginary 'God'! They found it easier to believe that 'God' and not they themselves and their higher energies, had created their lives!

They attributed 'God' with all their human emotions – of benevolence and tears and sympathy and their version of love. In hindsight, he realised, that people needed something to hold on to. They needed some way to explain the great mysteries of the universe that they were completely unable to grasp in its totality. A loving and caring form somewhere in the universe who hears their prayers and tears and delivers them from their fears was the answer. That being a physical era, the God either had a name and a family and a life story or He sent messengers and messiahs who had the life stories and then became humanity's only hope. Those gods and messengers then had messages that had to be followed to a 'T', there were rituals involved that kept one connected to the Gods and messengers and there were always those that were closer to these Gods than the common man, and they had further do's and do-not's on how to keep these gods happy. And that had created the religions.

It was hard to even imagine in today's day! The Science of the Soul was well documented today and people moulded their lives with the power of creation as it related to their energy levels. Even he – Skolt – had to consciously keep his mind in a flashback mode to describe those times long past because it was hard to explain those facts with today's mind-set. He could imagine how hard the youth must find it to understand what he said!

But the downside of keeping his mind there was that he lived the heart-wrenching pain of that life again.

The knife turned in his gut, and he was amazed at how easily he could feel the heart plexus act up. He was immediately restless and in pain for the young, loving woman he had been. It had been a turning point in his journey, and lately every time he visited that life, he felt the pain twist his heart again.

He should have been way beyond these emotions and anguish! And he was – usually.

The pain of an unrequited love that can wake up emotions hidden in a heart that had never loved and one that never loved like that again – can there be anything more painful? And he had understood that the reason he was born a woman in that life was to be able to give form to that emotion, to be able to feel the love in all its glory and pain. And that could only have been done by a woman in those times. Men would usually get on with life and had had to be practical. Such had been the priorities of that era.

Oh, the drama of it! Very well suited to the twenty-first century he felt. Or even better to the twentieth may be. But today? This era was heart-centric. It was normal to live with a well-activated heart plexus. It didn't require undue emotion, and absolutely no sentimentality existed. Along with the heart plexus, humans also had a very well-activated cerebral plexus. People were wise, considerate, and compassionate. They were all individuals, complete in their own ways, and no one person could penetrate another's aura, and neither did anyone ever have to, unless welcomed to. Language was in electric impulses that were telepathically communicated.

Communication was mostly non-verbal. Intentions and heart waves were read intuitively. Intuition was the use of the most basic of energies, which is to say it required the least effort. Music and dance had sound and voice but no words. Of course, there was a language and a script, but it was not used for everyday living. The basis of language today was a scientific sound-based structure, very like the old Sanskrit or Greek. The script was a version of Roman and Devanagari.

'Why a book on intelligence, Skolt? What possible importance could intelligence have on the human race? We associate intelligence and instinct with the animal kingdom, right?' asked a confused Danube.

'Danube! What do you think intelligence is? You know it was a very relevant concept for a number of centuries . . .'

'To absorb, retain, and eventually utilise knowledge productively would be an apt explanation of intelligence, I'd say. So why would we want to ask people to crowd their mind space with retaining knowledge?'

'Hmmm, that would be apt actually. So, are we intelligent human beings? Danube?' Skolt avoided answering the question just yet.

'Maybe . . . We've never really studied the human race on the basis of intelligence.'

Skolt looked at the lot of curious faces around him and smiled. This was his group of junior scholars. Eight highly evolved souls that were in his care from a very young age, and he hoped to mentor them to fully utilise their high energy frequency. How did one explain the need for intelligence to a heart-centred world that lived on intuition and sense connections?

'That's why we need to now. It's going to be very relevant very soon again.'

'Oh?'

'About 14,000 years ago, for a span of 5,000 years or so, the planet was a physical place – of matter and mass. Only the physical reality could be perceived. Man was born with only the kundalini plexus naturally stimulated. The kundalini plexus, as you know, is at the base of the spine and related to all things physical – to the material world so to speak. That was the prevalent energy level on the earth. Just enough to activate the kundalini plexus. Humans had a natural affinity or understanding of only physical reality. The heart plexus started to feature in the lives of the masses from the eighteenth-century CE as the Records show. People struggled and suffered and surrendered their higher energies in the name of love, not really knowing how the heart plexus would be activated or even that there was a heart plexus to activate. In fact, there used to be constant arguments over sex and love, and if one led to the other or if they both could exist independently and if there was even such a thing as love! The energy of the heart plexus was called love, even then, though the science of an activated heart plexus was not understood till a much later era.' Skolt paused.

'You're joking, of course!' said Holly. 'I don't see any record of that. People lived without a well-activated heart plexus? How did they live at all? How was it even possible?'

'Go really far back in the Akashics and look for "love". You'll find it. However impossible it sounds to all of you today, that was exactly how the heart plexus was uncovered, through a lot of pain and heartache that our ancestors lived with. It seems so natural to you now, but at one time it wasn't. And then the cerebral plexus – the soul-awakening? Wow! That came much, much later. Today, humans use all three plexus naturally. We don't really need to analyse the usage of body or heart or soul – that is, the kundalini plexus or heart plexus or cerebral plexus. Our pleasure and our functioning is a merging of all three energies. But at a time when energy came mostly from the kundalini plexus, when the heart plexus was not understood well enough to tap its potential and the cerebral plexus was non-functional, people had to juggle their happiness. They had to look for ways and means to keep life happy. They needed to be intelligent. They had to use their intelligence to find those ways. Though without a well-functioning heart plexus, the ways were usually way off base anyway. But they suited the purpose of growth well enough – therefore the discovery of money and marriage and family and power. These were all invented as means to be happy. And intelligent people, supposedly, handled their life well.'

'And were they happy?'

'Not usually. No', he had to admit, 'Of course, with the lack of the heart plexus, there was also overuse or abuse of the very discoveries that were supposed to bring happiness. But they were intelligent enough to know they were not happy, and they changed their course. Thus, a number of discoveries were made in those ancient times – which was a good outcome of their unhappiness.'

'But none of those discoveries actually made anyone happy, right?' Holly persisted.

'Not for any sufficient length of time, I guess. No.' Skolt sounded almost apologetic.

'Why couldn't they just look up the records and figure out the heart plexus? Why pretend an intelligence and suffer when you can just look it up?' Elina sounded confused.

'Hmmm . . . The Akashic records were not accessible then either.'

'Why not?!'

'Cerebral plexus was not activated then, Eli. Don't ask obvious questions!' The charming Danube answered. 'But what I don't understand, Skolt, is – why could they not just sense the heart plexus? That would be natural, right? So when you sense it and you follow it – ta-da! You're living it! How hard could that have been?'

'We . . . ee . . . ell,' Skolt hesitated and then bravely continued, 'their intelligence was the very attribute that blocked out the heart plexus waves!'

'Whaaat?!' All eight of them threw their energy at him, and he would have fallen over if he wasn't sitting firmly on his seat.

'Yes. And it truly was as complicated as it sounds actually. They needed their intelligence to survive and grow in that environment, but that very intelligence kept them removed from the energies of the heart plexus. At one point of time, it became almost like a standard understanding – one was either intelligent or emotional.'

There was a collective gasp from the room. He was sure they could not truly grasp the immenseness of the struggle humanity had gone through to balance these three energies. Their surprise came more from the thought of people actually living such a complex life. The humans of this 14,000th century took their pleasures for granted.

'By the standards of intelligence that were set in the ancient years, mankind today is the most intelligent it will ever be. And that is the cycle of intelligence the senior researchers are working on. The only reason we don't dwell on intelligence today is because we take it for granted. It just is. We don't need to know our level of intelligence, as it is not relevant in our lives. We call ourselves wise now. It is wisdom we use. Wisdom comes from routing our thoughts through the heart plexus and the universal soul energy and then acting upon the resultant thought. Centuries from now, mankind will say, 'the wise men of the 14,000th century . . . etc, etc, etc . . .' That would be you and me and our generation, by the way! We live from our heart plexus, and the physical and soul bodies all align with it. We don't notice the intelligence doing its job.' He looked at their physical forms and noticed the relaxed bodies in various sheetla positions, concentrating on his every word, and cut the discussion right there. 'Now pull out whatever you can on the topic of intelligence and help the paper along', Skolt concluded his talk and stood up.

And then as an afterthought, he added, 'And the next time you sit in sheetla try actually accessing the records rather than conversing with each other and *sukhsa-ing*!'

Skolt walked out of the room quite aware that the youngsters had paid no heed to that last statement of his. He shook his head at the simplicity of youth and smiled. There had never been a generation where the seniors didn't lament the state of the youth!

Even as Niti, he remembered the youngsters would constantly be occupied with a physical structure called the 'phone'. Not just the youth but at one time, the entire planet was obsessed with that connection gadget. People were constantly busy with that toy, and it would consume their days and years! Today, even though the youth did not need a physical gadget, they were still obsessed with connection. You would find people sitting around relaxed and in the sheetla pose everywhere, but very few would actually be doing something constructive. Most would just be connecting telepathically to others and could stay there for hours.

'Sukhsa' is the version of loving communication where it involves the heart plexus and the cerebral plexus, and lovers indulged in this emotional 'high' telepathically all the time. The level of pleasure is the same as a physical union would have been at the time that sex was all humans had, only, without the physical forms. Of course, the physical union is still the most coveted because it involved all three – the kundalini plexus, the heart plexus, and the cerebral plexus – and the pleasure is huge and way beyond expression. Enough to say you were in *tulsna*.

In fact, today, every action was sukhsa or 'making love' as the heart plexus was a part of everything. It didn't have a designated role where the heart was brought in to perform. The heart energy, or love, was a part of conversation, work, communication, relationships – everything. All action went from the heart plexus through the practicality of the cerebral plexus and into the human self. From within, as soul energy, the act was given form – either telepathic or electric or magnetic or physical. All actions were possible by the human form, and the entire process took about as long as it took a person to swallow food. There was no such thing as a 'wrong' action. The soul energy made no mistakes. Every act and every thought of every person deserved equal respect and so it was.

This was truly the golden era.

Today the only reason people come together for individual relationships is for energy exchange and growth. The concept of 'family' and 'marriage' that hearts had yearned for in the ancient past no longer existed. Marriages are created from the heart plexus when the individuals feel that the association will assist their soul growth. Marriage is not entered into to fill the gaps in life – financial or emotional or societal – and nor is it to have babies like it was at one time. In the distant past, as history shows, women were kept financially dependent and men were domestically challenged. Genders had specific roles. Marriages brought these incomplete lives together and the give and take of needs created a marriage. Love was only in so far as a willingness to live with one as opposed to any other. Children were meant to cement the bond in the long run and give the relationship a common goal.

Of course, over the course of the centuries, the tables turned, and in an attempt to make their place in society equal to men, women went overboard to the point where male–female relationships became a battlefield. It took many years of heart awakenings to find the balance that now existed.

Today marriage enhanced and added to an individual's life, and new life was created when individuals wanted or felt the deep need to create life. It was not a process of 'becoming complete'. Babies were usually brought up by the entire community because people lived in groups that were energy-synced. Similar energy beings usually gravitated together and built homes around a common base. They lived individual lives, but they lived in communities. That was the beauty of this era that the souls living in the twenty-first century would never have understood. The oneness of humanity is intrinsically lived. People are always close to each other telepathically and always felt complete and content. Everyone lived on earth using their share of the resources as required and helped others using whatever inherent talent one chose to work with at any given point of time.

He remembered the living conditions that had gone high up into the air in the past. People had used up all the land on earth and had started using air space for living! Wow! Where would the world have gone if that had continued? The need to posses more of everything had been the driving force of that time.

But the universe and the higher energies know best, of course. The great calamity of the 7,600th century had destroyed most everything. The water had risen above ground level, and new topography had emerged. Countries and continents today were very different from what they were 12,000 years ago. Fortunately, the planet had been revived.

Strange how he had always chosen the Hind Kush area to take birth in the past! Not this time, though. Yes, he was partial to that side of the planet. The area that had then been known as India. And why not? Most of his understandings of the working of this universe had come from being exposed to the vibrations of that area. The Hindu Kush even today carried the most number of growing souls, even though it was mostly water now.

'Hmmm,' reflected Skolt. Never was anything wasted. Every act of nature, however devastating, had a purpose. And yet, at times, it had felt like he had wasted lifetimes. He could have accomplished all that he had to, in half the number of lifetimes, but he had muddled through so many more. Oh, the naivety of a young soul!

The ache hadn't left him. As much as he liked to pretend, he obviously wasn't over it yet. Back on the planet Earth twice after that life, he had brought about tremendous changes in the energies of the planet. He understood his journey well, and all the supposed pain and struggle of his heart plexus was perfectly explained by science. And yet . . .

Skolt walked into the hall at the community living site he shared with other members of his energy level. He had closed his mind's energy so as not to receive any messages telepathically. He had also cloaked his aura, hoping that his restlessness didn't cause too much damage to the people around him. Even with the cloak of blockage around him, he could sense the flow of energy coming at him as he walked up to his room.

As with most people of this era, Skolt was tall and well built and lived in a healthy body. There was nothing different or exceptional in that. The attributes that demanded attention in this world were the energy levels. The physical, emotional, and mental energies were the most attractive features of humans. The entire mating game today was about energy connections. And Skolt's energy attracted everyone he met. There was not one born who could resist the man, it was said, in the senior circles.

Skolt was aware of this fact, of course, but his focus on his purpose for this particular lifetime was so complete that nothing could seem to distract him. Lara had come close, but she had read his intent and felt his commitment to his purpose, and it didn't go with her energies, so, of course, they had moved on.

His big work of this lifetime was to get these comparison documents done, as they would be preserved for posterity and be the resource for the planet when it went into its dark phase again and people struggled to understand their world. He was, after all, the memory keeper. He knew there were a few thousand years yet before *Kalyuga* was upon the human race again, but as the downward cycle had started, he needed to get the work done. The ability to grasp knowledge would only recede from here, and intelligence would become an obstacle to growth again. Maybe commissioning these books would in itself be the start of these concepts!

Duality – thy name is nature!

Which meant that he had to keep his mental-mode on the past and stay in the CE years. Which meant that there was no escaping his thoughts!

Nothing had ever deterred him from his path. Not in the last lifetime as Kalki and not in this lifetime, as yet. But he could feel something pulling at him. Was it time? Was he going to achieve fulfilment of the dreams and desires that he had so prayed for so many centuries ago? The dreams that he had accepted as impossible and the desires that he had given different names to? Was it to be? Now, finally?

The thrill that ran through him proved more than anything else that he had never really accepted those dreams as impossible, and the desires had never really changed names. They lay within him still – as fresh and aching as ever.

Yes, he did believe the time had come. He had to lay ghosts to rest.

'What does it look like, Hoyt?' Skolt hoped his energies stayed stable through this very important meeting. He needed to focus. This was the senior research group, and they were working on his document 'The Book of Intelligence'.

'We're still exploring . . .' Hoyt's telepathic reply sounded normal and his usual self. Not like he was startled or anything – which meant that Skolt had managed to control his wayward energies.

'Anything that comes to mind that you may want to talk about?' Skolt persisted. He had sensed that the group had reached a roadblock.

The five researchers sat in this beautiful glade in different states of sheetla, accessing the Akashic Records, saving or rejecting information as was required and simultaneously discussing and copying it out into the ether, all non-verbal communications but requiring a lot of energy and concentration. Hoyt was the typical focused science mind that no energy could penetrate. He only gave out telepathic energy when he was pushed to. Skolt assumed that Hoyt would have to come back in a different era where his heart plexus could know pain and merge more fully with the other plexus. But for now he was needed here.

'Well . . ., there is this one thing . . .' Skolt felt Hoyt's hesitation. He knew Hoyt didn't really want to talk about it because Hoyt would love to solve the puzzle on his own – which he obviously could have, as it existed in the ether and would eventually surface, but Skolt didn't want to wait that long. He had other papers to create after this.

'You're going to have to allow me to read your energy or just put it out there for me to scan, Hoyt.'

'Intelligence grows', Hoyt started abruptly. 'Man uses almost 100 per cent of his brain capacity at one point, as we do now, but we have come to this from a point where man was unable to use more than 25 per cent of his brain. Today we've gone beyond intelligence even. But . . . what causes this brain potential growth?'

'That's significant data right there. Can you verify intellectual brain capacity growth?'

'Well, we know we use from 80 to 100 per cent of our brain potential. There are writings and tests performed on human "specimens" in the last 8,000 years that show brain potential usage of 70 per cent and 50 per cent and as low as 40 per cent. And then I just chanced upon texts from the nineteenth century that said human specimens then used merely 25 per cent of their brain capacity! Whew! That low . . . !'

'There will be no record of less than that because at that level of brain development, humans wouldn't know to test their brains!' They all laughed indulgently – if a little distractedly.

'Usage of brain capacity is directly proportional to intellect. But increasing intellect doesn't cause brain potential to increase.' Hoyt's mental energy was almost musing.

'By being more knowledgeable or more intelligent, as the ancient humans chose to view themselves, brain capacity does not grow, but with an increase in brain potential, more knowledge can be stored and people would be considered more intelligent', Janice, the meticulous one, put the thought into a recognisable scientific statement.

'Don't forget areas of "intelligence"', Skolt prodded. 'When humans had reduced brain potential, they also did not have a well-activated heart plexus. There was no heart intelligence, only brain.'

'What does the heart plexus have to do with intelligence?'

'When you don't have a working heart plexus, the intellect is all important. And at that time, humans were using only 25 per cent of brain capacity? Seems to be hugely short-changed, doesn't it? And we know the universe doesn't work that way. Unless . . . the reason the heart plexus didn't activate was the lack of brain potential.'

There was an immediate stillness in energy levels. Suddenly all brains were working to 100 per cent capacity!

'What would cause the brain to work at only 25 per cent or only 40 per cent, and what would cause it to move from one level to the next? Not aggregation of knowledge. Not intellectual capacity. Then what?'

'Kiera, have you done a time scan on the levels of intelligence? You *are* doing the timelines, right?' Turning to the group at large, Skolt continued, 'Research that will eventually cover 48,000 years will need detailed timeline preservation. Else you will never find the thread.'

'Yes, I am, Skolt. I realise your mention of 48,000 years has a number of cycles of various events that can have occurred, but we have to see which cycle of events this phenomenon coincides with.'

'Precisely! And the cycle should show perfect repetitive patterns and be consistent before we can take it to the council.

One cycle of 48,000 years is not enough. So don't look at big cycles. Look at smaller ones.'

'Hmmm . . . the rise of brain potential. What on earth would cause that?' Skolt took his thoughts forward. Intellect was incidental to the brain potential capacity, and something outside of human control caused the change. It had to obviously be an element of nature or a phenomenon of nature that caused this variation. Like day and night. Or summer and winter. Or magnetic polarisation.

That's right! That was exactly it!

'You're right, Skolt!' exclaimed Hoyt. In his excitement, Skolt had removed the barrier to his thoughts, and his team could access the energies he was giving out. And Hoyt had read him immediately.

'That's what it must be. A nature's phenomenon or a natural element that caused these changes.'

'It would have been so much easier if we were living in the ancient years. We could have just passed it all on to 'God'! That 'God' gave brain capacity – as much or as little as He chose to, and it needn't have any scientific basis. So there!' mimicked the exasperated Dorothy who was a keen researcher but a keener outdoorsy person. She loved doing things in her own time, and being on a time clock like this was alien and difficult for her. She was the original free spirit.

'The higher energies of the universe might have something to say about that, Dorothy', laughed Skolt along with the others.

The momentary reprieve put everyone back in the mood for answers, and the study got underway again.

Skolt walked out as abruptly as he had come there. No one paid any attention. They were always connected telepathically anyway. It was just that Skolt had closed his mental reception and so had come to them for a close-distance communication. The fact that no one mentioned that he had been untraceable for more than a day showed that they hadn't tried to get in touch with him either.

This was not a good time to be distracted, he rued. His entire soul journey had been leading up to this all-important work entrusted to him by the higher energies as it was to be their earth support structure for eons to come, and he had waited forever to be able to start it. And now that he had, it seemed to have opened the floodgates to other things that he had apparently been waiting to experience.

My Word   2016 CE
                                                        India

Energy is the currency of the soul.

It doesn't matter a whit if you believe in the soul or not. You are a soul being, and if the universe had to wait its manifestation on man's acceptance of universal laws, we would be living on a flat, square world. Fortunately, the universe moves on undisturbed by man's supercilious beliefs.

Our life on earth is nothing more than the journey of this soul to reach its highest possible frequency. No benevolent God, no mythological creature, no messenger, no saint, and no guru is beyond this journey. This journey is all there is. And the ones who claim to preach can do no better than help you see this journey.

Reason and intellect being strong in this twenty-first century as compared to even two centuries ago, man is perfectly capable of understanding this journey on his own and following through. All else will be a waste.

So, energy is the currency of the soul. It flows through the body through *nadis* just like blood flows through arteries and veins.

Any action, thought, idea, or mental activity you indulge in will create energy. While some energy will be used in the act to create more energy, eventually energies will begin to accumulate and grow. The energy is stored in the astral body or energy body that is the inner body to the outer physical form. This astral body houses the 'chakras', which are nothing but energy plateaus and the chakras are connected through nadis. The chakras are 'safe houses' of energy.

*refer to image on page 26

Man's energy at the beginning of his soul journey in human form is concentrated in the lowest chakra at the base of his spine and it activates the kundalini plexus. As human acts/thoughts/intentions/efforts generate energy, the nadis carry the surplus energy up the spinal cord towards the next chakra that resides behind the naval and then higher to the next and so forth. During the course of this journey, which can take many lifetimes or maybe one swift quantum leap, energy is added and depleted depending on the human journey. There are seven chakras along the spinal cord.

When energy has been collected to a particular quantum level, which would coincide with a particular chakra, it reaches a 'safe house'. Like video game energy forms, any give and take of energy henceforth cannot take you below the level of that particular 'safe house'. Even if the person dies the astral body with the soul energy, remains steady. The next physical form the soul takes will have spiritual energy at that particular level and will grow from there. Your spiritual efforts are never in vain. It is the only thing that outlasts death – the soul and the soul energy.

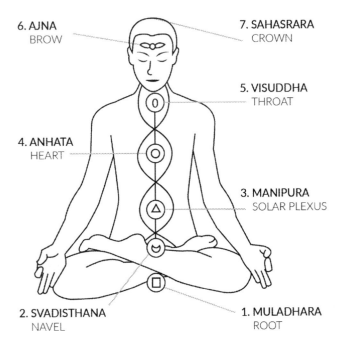

6. AJNA
BROW

7. SAHASRARA
CROWN

5. VISUDDHA
THROAT

4. ANHATA
HEART

3. MANIPURA
SOLAR PLEXUS

2. SVADISTHANA
NAVEL

1. MULADHARA
ROOT

In the human form it takes the soul a long time to move from the lowest point of the spectrum, the kundalini plexus, to the point where it can merge with the higher energy plane, the cerebral plexus. To accomplish this, the soul needs to take human form again and again till it gathers the required energy. Accumulation of sufficient energy causes the heart plexus to open first.

The heart plexus connects the human body to the energy body and the cerebral plexus connects these two to the soul body. Chakras reflect their energy through the physical body but the concept of manipulating these chakras for 'better living', as is common place today, is not true. Nothing, but nothing can alter your chakra or its energy and growth other than your inner energy. And that can only come *from* better living and not the other way around. The chakras are never 'misaligned'. They are never weak. They merely correspond to the activities and life of the human form. All one has to do to have a healthy, happy soul growth is to focus on a happy, healthy soul growth. Indulging in manipulation of the chakras or pranic[1] energy will never, never yield the result needed for the ultimate purpose of your existence. Only you – your actions, your beliefs and your connection with your source – can bring about any permanent changes in your life.

The chakra coinciding with the heart plexus is a huge plateau of energy and a person may be stuck there for lifetimes and not move on. Simply because energy generation requires intelligence as well as wisdom as well as sufficient emotion but the heart chakra generates an abundance of emotion and can keep humans locked in its romantic, sentimental warmth, which keeps them from attempting to break that comfort zone. Not till one has passed the heart chakra and moved beyond, can the heart plexus be activated.

The soul is continuously gathering energy. It is adding energy to itself. It is continuously being pulled by the presence of a higher energy around it and it is continuously aspiring to that energy level, to that vibrational level, to that frequency. This clamouring will not end till the soul vibrates at the highest frequency it can sense, whether you believe one thing or the other. You want to call it re-incarnation? Go ahead. The point is – the soul has always been looking for a higher energy to move to and it will continue to do so through various forms and shapes. These may be lifetimes to you, but to the soul they are only a ladder of frequencies it is climbing.

The soul needs to gather enough energy to vibrate at the highest level. That energy can only be gathered in human form through action and intent. The soul *has* to take human form to accomplish its goal. To be human and act and will as human is the only, only thing one needs to do.

All the restlessness in life and the yearnings of human life are merely the soul's calls to move on and gather energy. Only humans get 'bored'. This is because the soul needs food. It needs energy. Sometimes it is in a place that is not adding to its energy level, sometimes it is in a body that is not working towards energy gathering. The soul constantly needs energy addition. It needs to grow.

The soul gathers energy in any number of ways.

The Karma Way

The Upanishads[1] believed, as was believed by Adi Shankaracharya[2], that 'Karma' is a necessary fiction.

'Good actions' is a way for the soul to gather energy. It's actually equivalent to small change in terms of energy currency, but it's where we all start from.

Every soul and every event in your life is an opportunity to create energy. If you overcome, open your heart and live, find joy and laughter, include, embrace and generally live a life of 'bigness' you add energy to your life. If you live in anger, resentment, hatred, gossip, stress and generally everything that closes your heart you lose energy. Your choice of how you want to be at any point of your life is your karma. You can live for your soul or you can live for society. Your choice. Always your choice.

The definition of 'good' changes with every generation and is a hugely controversial term. Good actions as in the 'intent' is what was meant and not enforced 'good' actions. To make sure humans get to even this minimal point of loose change, karma, as a theory, was proposed and it was assumed that man would get onto the path of 'right action', 'right work' and would eventually evolve onto the soul path from there. (Today, of course, it seems like we are stuck with good and right and positive and all other moralistic definitions and we refuse to move to the soul path!) Being able to perform your actions for reasons bigger than name, fame, glory and money would be following the soul path.

Break the Comfort-Zone

In short: Any action that has you looking up at the heavens above and asking for strength is generating soul energy.

Every time one moves out of one's comfort zone, takes risks or strives for more than the limits of one's mind, they generate soul energy. Any action that has you stretching your limits – of endurance or understanding or compassion or finance or creativity – will invariably generate soul energy.

Actions that generate a sense of fear in oneself or in another will drain soul energy from your reserve. Anger, lack of self-control, aggression and monotony are huge spenders of this energy. The strength to overcome bad life situations, monotony and societal pressure cannot be found in any process outside of you. It can only come when you connect with the energy within you and learn how to use it. To believe that the world is separate from you, your mental health is separate issue or that your circumstances are for any reason other than your growth is the very reason we look outside for answers. No. Everything is connected to us from within. We need to get within. Only then will medicines affect us best if we need them at all. Only then can we alter situations around us. We owe allegiance to our soul first and foremost.

Love and Happiness ☺

Chapter 2

Considering how much she had been looking forward to this break, she could have been more organised! Damn! She needed to be more organised. Period.

It was a 6.20 a.m. flight and she needed to be at the airport at 5.20 a.m. at least. It was 5 a.m. already. Though she was barely ten minutes from the airport, the traffic even at this hour looked bad. She had been sitting in this jam for twenty minutes and who knew how long it would take to get out of it.

No, no, no! She had wanted so badly to go on this off-site with the team. She could cry just about now, thought Niti in despair. And it wasn't like she hadn't been warned.

'Leave the house by four, Niti. The international airport is like a shopping mall at Diwali, all night', Divyansh had said. And she had laughed.

'Idiot!' she cursed herself.

'Come on, come on, come on', she prayed under her breath. 'Any gods, angels, guides, listening to me around here? Please, please, please make this trip happen. I've had a bitch of a month at work. Oops, sorry! Forgive the language. But I have had a hard time and you know that, right, God?' Niti tapped her foot and looked out of all the windows of the cab, expecting to find a way out. She kept up a continuous 'oh God' chant that was making the cabbie nervous too.

'Can't you work your magic, God? May the traffic part and the flight be late,' Niti commanded under her breath, not for a moment expecting anything to happen.

She pulled out her mobile phone and sent out messages to her friends – desperate, praying, whining messages. There were a flurry of responses, and she kept replying to each. Oooh! They had all checked in! She was going to miss this!

'Madam, I think you should get off here and run!' The cabbie's voice sounded almost as anxious as her inner voice. Niti looked up and noticed that they had gotten out of that jam and were very close to the airport entrance, but the cars were lined up a mile long at the drop off point. Yes! Get off and run! She had just the one bag. Yes, yes, yes! She just might make it!

Yelling into her phone for her friends to wait, paying the cabbie and making to dash into the airport all at the same time, Niti landed at the check-in with a crash – her hair all over the place and almost tripping over her own luggage and her feet.

Her friends met her there with squeals of excitement, helping her check-in and cursing her happily for being late simultaneously. With a lot of noise and amid complete ruckus the motley group ran towards security check and their boarding gates.

Ye . . . es, that's what Indians are famous for.

The noise and confusion?

No.

The exuberant living. OK . . ., noisy, exuberant living.

'You're Niti Chaddha, aren't you?'

The sane, quiet voice belonged to the man standing in the boarding line next to hers. He wasn't in her line of vision, and she was amazed she had even heard him amid all the noise her group was making and the airport announcements.

She turned to look, but before she could see who the person was, he continued, 'I'm Salil Reza. We went to college together . . . ?'

Niti froze in mid-turn. Salil Reza? From college he had said. The hugely popular president of the college council? The Salil Reza of batch '90? It was always exciting to meet alumni. And a college personality type . . . ? Wow!

Niti finished her turnabout with extra vigour and almost landed at his feet. With a big, happy smile she greeted him, 'Hi!'

'Hi!'

'Of course, I remember you. You were president of the college council, right? Did you know of me in college? I don't think we'd met . . . ?' Niti turned to show the attendant her pass. 'You were a batch senior. Of course, I had heard of you . . . and seen you. I mean, who hadn't? In college, that is . . .'

Shut up, girl, shut up. He might want to say something.

'I'm surprised you recognised me.' Niti's voice slowly dwindled into silence. He didn't look like he wanted to say something. She felt uncomfortable in his silent presence. He could return the enthusiasm; after all it was he who had brought up the college connection.

He could fidget at the least!

'Yes, you were a junior. One batch, was it? I don't know how I recognised you – I'm good with faces and names, I guess', he finally said.

Niti smiled at him vaguely. Salil grinned back. He knew she had expected some fantastical explanation of how memorable she had been in college or some such girly fluff, but seriously, no. He just happened to make the connection

when her friends kept calling her name. And he *was* good with
names and faces.

She greeted the flight attendant as she entered the plane.
Salil followed right behind, still not saying a word.

She found her seat and turned to him. He looked at the
number of her seat, nodded at her, and said, 'We'll catch up
later,' and walked on.

That's it.

That's it?

That's why he had said *hi*? To be able to keep quiet and
walk on? WT . . . ?

Jerk. He could have at least made polite conversation.
It had been all of – she checked her watch – a seven-minute
walk. The least he could have done was, well, more than that.

The snoot!

She hoped he was on the wrong flight and they threw him
out. Right about now would be good thank-you.

She looked around hopefully, but, of course, there was no
drama taking place. Travellers were creeping along the aisle
and seating themselves. The usual pre-take-off stuff.

'Friendly fellow . . . ', mumbled Debbie sarcastically under
her breath.

Niti shook her head as if to shake off the meeting and
turned back to her friends with a smile. She was sitting a few
rows behind them because she had checked in later, so they
tried juggling seats but couldn't manage to get seats together.
Niti happily settled into her window seat alone knowing she
was going to sleep through the flight anyway. She'd had a
hectic morning. And it was barely 6 a.m. yet!

Her first holiday in six months. She deserved this were Niti's last thoughts as she drifted off to sleep a couple of minutes later.

'Hey! You asleep?'

She woke with a start and looked at the man in the seat next to her. Salil. She blinked a few dozen times, feeling quite disoriented and also quite sure that there had been some other man in the seat when she had fallen asleep at take-off.

'I changed seats with the guy sitting here', Salil said calmly as if replying to a question. It was obviously written on her face. 'I thought we'd catch up.'

'Catch up?'

'There was too much noise earlier. I'd have had to shout to be heard. It's better now. Easier to talk and hear.' He settled himself more comfortably in his seat.

'Easier? Even though I was asleep?' She hoped she sounded as affronted as she felt.

'Were you really asleep? Oh, I'm so sorry. Sorry! I thought you were just . . . You want to go back to sleep? It's OK with me.'

'No. No, it's OK. I don't think I could, even if I wanted to now.' And now she probably sounded sulky. 'But that's what you get when you mess with me at 6.30 a.m.', she thought.

Conversation started hesitantly till they found common friends and acquaintances to talk about and then college memories to laugh about and then a little about each other. She found out that he was in the middle of a divorce and worked as the marketing head for an e-retail company. He was currently posted in Delhi but was looking to make manager – Asia/Pacific and would then move to Singapore.

He sounded surprised that she wasn't married with kids at the age of thirty-five.

'Almost got married once. But I came to my senses just in time', she grinned at him.

'Are you anti-men? Or any other newer term that I haven't heard about?'

'No. And I'm not lesbian either.'

'So you're single and happy. Boyfriend?'

'Now and then. No one currently.'

He looked at her intently, as if to see if she was genuinely happy or faking it, she assumed. It was the year 2003 and India was still waking up to single women. People were still unsure about what to say to a single woman that would not offend her! And Salil too stayed quiet for a minute to absorb the news.

And then he noticed the book she was reading, and they started talking about books and authors and their opinions on everything.

Before she knew it, the two-and-a-half-hour flight was almost over, and the captain announced their landing in Goa. Niti and Salil had exchanged phone numbers, and even though they were staying at different beaches and quite a distance from each other, they'd decided to meet up at least one evening in the week that she was there. Salil was going to be there for a while. He was conducting two week-long conferences back to back and then taking a short break before heading back.

They made their way down the aisle and reached baggage claim where Niti's friends were waiting for her. Niti made the introductions and there were rounds of hi's and bye's and nice-meeting-you's and suddenly she was out in the bright Goa sun. Holiday time!

'Not typically handsome', commented Debbie. She always had something to say.

'No. But he's interesting. Easy to talk to. Come to think about it, we got on fantastically! I wasn't bored or pissed off even once! Hmm!'

And then she stopped thinking about it and the fun began! The Great Goan Holiday! They had the most amazing time – the beer, the beach, the parties, and the company! There wasn't a moment when something crazy wasn't happening. She hadn't laughed this much in ages!

Her friends envied her freedom because they were all tied down with husbands and children, and even in Goa every one of them had to have at least two calls home every day either to check up or check in or just say hi! But Niti didn't have a care in the world, and she wouldn't have it any other way. If she had ever thought about it, she would have wondered why she never felt the craving for home and family. She was never home sick for her parent's home and she never regretted not getting married and having a home of her own. Why, you'd think, wouldn't you? But Niti had never thought about it. She lived life to her heart's content. Getting into a relationship or not was never a huge decision for her. If she liked the guy things would move on, if she didn't she said bye. She never worried about it. She never thought she had to hold on. And it never took her more than a month to get over a relationship when it was over.

Now that Skolt thought about it, he realised that the fact that nothing affected her deeply was because her heart plexus was safely closed. There was just enough energy to fan the plexus into initial feelings, which were always superficially good. Most people lived like that in that era. But this had been the lifetime chosen to open her heart plexus. Oh, the little love! If only she knew what was waiting for her . . .

Chapter 3

'You seem to have found something interesting Elina. Or at least the feel of your energies says "interesting". Or is it "confusing"?'

'I don't know, Skolt. I'm thinking maybe I can't find the link. Maybe I need more research.'

'Why don't you share it with us?'

'So, I was reading up on the intelligence thing and I came across one Darwin Theory that spoke about the evolution of the species. I could follow what he was trying to say. But suddenly – I can't say – but I think he got it all wrong. I just can't seem to find the link that will make his theory sync.'

Ah! The evolution of the species, yes. Huge gaps there, he knew. That was to be his next research paper because it was going to involve research into millions of years and not just thousands. Too soon for the young ones to be looking into that. But anyway, no harm in getting them started.

'What did you think was missing? What would you be looking for?'

'I had come upon the Darwin Theory too. I rejected it as spam though. It made no sense at all to me', piped in Danube.

'Oh? Why don't we discuss it?' said Skolt settling into a seat.

'Well . . .' started Elina, 'He does talk about the journey starting at a unicellular level and evolving physically into more complex structures based on the need to adapt to the environment. While that is true . . .'

'Really? What's true about that?' interrupted Danube.

Skolt knew what was coming. It had been a debate for centuries.

'I haven't finished yet, Danube!' rushed in Elina.

'To continue – while it's true that complex beings come from unicellular beginnings, it is not possible that the growth occurs due to adaptations for survival. Because unicellular creatures still survive. If the environment sustains one it can sustain a million. Why would some cells need to adapt and not others? Obviously mutation for survival cannot be the core reason for evolution.'

'And it's not. We all know that. That's why the guy's spam!'

'And that's why I feel I need to find more of his research. Probably where he talks about the energy growth of living things? I'm thinking maybe he's done it in two volumes. One about the physical changes and one about energy. Obviously the energy one would be the first but I can't seem to find it and I don't find mention of it in this one either. Weird, right?'

Skolt took a deep breath. He was feeling an affinity to his Niti lifetime lately and he didn't like talking about the ignorance of that era. It felt almost personal! But then . . .

'There is no other volume.'

'No?!'

'I told you! The guy's spam.'

'Oh keep quiet Danube! He may have died before he could finish his research. This stuff takes years. Is that what happened Skolt?' Holly the pacifier.

'Well, I don't really know how long he lived after he published his paper. You can find that in his bio. But I do know that his paper was the basis of the understanding for evolution for the longest time. Most of the nomenclature we use even today to classify flora and fauna is derived from the structure based on Darwin's theory. Later, the Darwin Theory became the base point for further understanding and elaborate changes were made to the evolution concept. To the point where today, evolution theories bear no resemblance to Darwin's original theory.

'You have to understand that the concept of living beings being largely energy beings was not predominant in those days. Like I told you earlier, only the Kundalini Plexus was activated. Man was mostly a physical creature. All that he could see and quantify was true for him. So he focused only on the physical changes and the obvious differences in living things. That was all that he could relate to. The Darwin Theory was a reflection of its times.'

'You're saying that they didn't know that a unicellular organism has a soul and as the soul gathers energy it propels the physical form to disintegrate and re-create itself in higher energy forms continuously till it finally comes into the human form and spends lifetimes raising its energy, creating and re-creating human forms in different environments and different eras so as to reach the energy level of the universe and move into the higher energy sphere? They didn't know that the template for all forms has always existed in the ether and every soul that achieves a particular energy level takes on a template of that energy form?' Incredulous energy burst out of the group.

'They didn't even know that inanimate, plant and animate beings were all linked together with the same soul energy!' Skolt added to their incredulousness. 'They knew there was *some* connection and the physical chain solved the puzzle. But beyond that there was no knowledge of oneness during the Darwin era. That came much later.'

'So they didn't know that not species as a whole, but every soul as an individual has been through this path of evolution to be born human? That every human today was once an inanimate mound of dust that gathered energy and took plant form and then animal form and then human form?!'

'How did they create affinity with the other forms of nature and the elements if they could not see themselves in it?'

'Yes, that was a tough one for a long while there. Humans destroyed nature and abused animals, not knowing the true nature of evolution of the soul. They focused merely on evolution of the species and assumed that man was the most superior species. Most complicated.'

'Superior?!?'

'As in more intelligent. Able to reason and create.'

'We're all just souls in progress. We're all growing. Some have more energy than others but that's not a superior thing, surely? The only thing that establishes our seniority energy-wise is our wisdom, and destroying nature and animals does not display wisdom.'

'How it must have hurt the lower energy souls trying so hard to absorb higher energies. It probably delayed the growth of the smaller souls too, didn't it?' A sad, gloomy atmosphere was falling over the group. They could almost feel the pain of the souls who had suffered at the hands of the ignorant so long ago.

'Can you imagine how we would feel if the higher energies of the universe chose to hurt us? Or abandon us? Or even if they ignored us?' the group shuddered at Holly's words.

'Oh! How terribly, terribly sad!' Isabella rarely shared her thoughts but her cry came clearly through this time.

Now look what you've done Darwin, thought Skolt.

'And all because one guy didn't think his research through!' Danube sounded annoyed. He had been moved too now, had he?

'And you Danube, are doing exactly what mankind did 12,000 years ago. As are the rest of you.'

The group looked at Skolt in surprise.

'You have knowledge and you have wisdom. Knowledge tells you that the soul takes time and experience and needs the physical form to generate energy for growth. Knowledge also tells you that the soul will grow at its own pace and will act in correspondence with the energy it has. Your wisdom should then show you why mankind did what it did. They were evolving too. Their energies were at a lower rung, around the kundalini plexus only. They didn't have the ability to grasp or understand their limitations or the complexities of the soul. They were in the process of growth too. Because they stumbled and grew, you and I today, are far more evolved. We were those people then and we were the abused souls then. But we all turned out OK, right? We're all good, right? So no harm done. Just part of the journey of evolution.'

Silence. Oh ho! He had actually brought this group to silence! That had to be a first.

And then the energies all came bursting at him all at once. They got it. They were happy again. This made perfect sense. They had gotten back their connection to the past and their connection to the higher energies in the future too. They were good. They were going to be OK!

'Next time you're in Sheetla, try and find a lifetime of your own in that era. It will help you connect better.'

'And Darwin?'

'We'll do a paper on him next and rip apart his theory if it'll make you people feel better.'

They smiled at him but they had got their affinity and benevolence back. They didn't want to rip anyone apart anymore. But they would want to dig out more knowledge.

He knew that. After all this was the era for that. Knowledge refurbishing and consolidation.

'Hoyt?' Skolt sent out a message to Hoyt as he walked out of the room and into the clear, crisp morning on his way to his home.

'Hoyt?'

'Yes Skolt. We're in the research facility. Room 4.'

'No, I'm not coming in but I have an angle that I want the lot of you to look into.' Immediately the others were in the conversation and he could feel their energies as though they had logged onto a computer of yesteryears.

'Go on Skolt?'

'A lack of brain potential could mean the inability to understand completely the ways of the universe. We have proof – and I want you to pull it out and state it – that humans 12,000 years ago were not aware of the energy body and the heart plexus that connected it to the physical body. And 10,000 years ago, while people were aware of the heart plexus and the energy body, they were still not aware of the cerebral plexus and the soul body. They could not connect with higher energies or build communication between their physical and soul bodies internally.'

'Yes, but that is a well documented fact. What do you want us to do with it?'

'Not to understand the ways of the universe is one thing. But suppose – they didn't understand because it didn't exist!'

'What didn't exist? The universe!'

'What are you talking about, Skolt?'

'Whaatt?'

'OK, OK. Let me explain it to you in detail.' Skolt sat down under a tree and composed his thoughts.

'14,000 years ago, when Kalyuga was upon us, it is said that it was the darkest age of mankind. It was a physical world and man could grasp nothing more than that which he could see and touch and taste. We say his brain potential was merely 25 per cent. So, can't it be that the souls evolving into human form from animal form choose this yuga to come in as it does not require too much work from them to adjust and learn? Souls that land on the human plane initially only have enough energy to activate their kundalini plexus – which is what we see till about 1700 CE. Not only did they not have enough soul energy to activate the heart plexus, they didn't have the brain capacity to understand the heart plexus either. Their actions and intents and lifetimes on earth, consequently, produce progressively evolved souls to the point that the energy of the earth supports higher energy beings which then start to take birth and live out their lives and who have their heart plexus partially open and that helps all the beings on earth get to a place of recognising and understanding the heart plexus and the energy bodies. And once the soul energy on the planet is sufficiently raised the cerebral plexus comes into play and beings that need physical form to activate their cerebral plexus and soul connections start to take birth and the energy continues to grow till it reaches the level we are at.'

Skolt stopped to collect his thoughts and think through what he'd just telepathised to the team.

'Wait Skolt, wait . . .'

He could sense each one of them putting the facts into their own kind of order to grasp it better. Before they decided to accept or reject it, he assumed.

'OK. Take your time and think it through. Whether you accept or reject the theory, I want proof to justify your decision. Each one of you individually. Comprehensive proof.'

'Wait, Skolt!' That was Hoyt. 'You're saying, instead of studying the wave of intelligence growth we should be studying the journey of soul evolution and energy? But I thought the whole point was a study of intelligence. Isn't this a whole different concept?'

'It could be. But like we said yesterday, something was causing the growth of brain potential and it was outside the control of humans. Maybe the two are related? In fact, I'm quite sure the two are related I just need some of you to agree enough to dig out the data, chronicle it and put it into a scientific paper kind of language.'

Skolt send them a laughing energy and signed out.

He was ecstatic. It felt good after wallowing in Niti's pain for the last few days. But she would be back. He knew she would.

And Salil did actually call. A couple of days into the Goa holiday and he called to say he was giving his team the evening off and he was free. He said he knew a lovely Greek restaurant overlooking the beach, if she was interested? She was, she said. And they decided to meet at the restaurant.

'He's not even cute! Why would you back out of the beach party to go with Him?'

'I thought you said he wasn't handsome?' replied Niti uninterestedly while finishing getting dressed.

'Not handsome and not even cute!'

'Hmmm.'

'What hmmm? Is that how you want to spend even one evening in glorious Goa? Waste it?'

'I'm quite looking forward to the evening, Debbie. He's interesting.'

And he was. She didn't really know why but she was kind of excited about the evening. She had a feeling she was going to have a good time. Good conversation, good food ... What more was there to ask for?

Oh no, no, no, no, no . . . Skolt thought. Don't go! He wanted to go right up to her and warn her. 'Fuck him if you want to, but don't talk to him', Skolt wanted to say. Don't let him get into your head!

But, of course, he didn't say anything. And, of course, she went. And, of course, she had the most marvellous time! They talked and laughed. Despite a lot of things in common, they had enough differences for arguments to break out at regular intervals. It was fun. The food must have been good too. She couldn't honestly say what it had tasted like but she hadn't balked at any time of the night so it must have been OK.

She came back to her hotel with a highly massaged brain and quite happy to know that there were well read and matured men her age still around. She always settled for the older ones as they seemed more mature but were invariably boring. But not Salil. He was himself. And himself was not boring at all.

He had dropped her to the coffee shop where the rest of her friends were, at that time of the night. He had sat around for a while and then said he had an early start the next day, said bye to everyone, thanked her for a lovely evening and left.

Nice. Very nice. She was happy!

The rest of the Goa holiday continued just the way it had started. She thought of Salil intermittently but not seriously. She was having a good time.

That's what you think! Skolt wanted to shake her till she broke something so she could feel something, anything, deeply enough that it would not require deep pain to open her heart plexus.

Looking from his new perspective, he knew he had to first be made to feel love and then to feel the heart break. Slowly, bit by bit, till it was completely split open. And then it was up to him how he filled the heart plexus. With soul energy or bitterness or anger. Any process would eventually lead only to soul energy, it was just that one usually started with the painful ways and the journey to soul energy was that much longer and painful.

'Love', as was commonly understood at that time didn't even skim the top of the emotions the heart plexus could feel. People in those days still debated on whether there was any such thing as true love! And in India, where Niti lived, even if love did exist, it was meant for the foolish youth. No one who claimed to be 'grown-up' would give love more importance than society and family and responsibilities. Love was another word for compromise or adjustments or acceptance or whatever.

If only the heart plexus had been opened, there would have been no question. The true depth of emotion would have been so great that debate would never have occurred. Partners, families and businesses would all have come together and stayed together because of the true energy of the heart plexus. They would have completed their immediate connection and moved on with their journey also because of the depth of feeling. No sense of abandonment or rejection would ever have prevailed.

But sadly, it wasn't time for that yet. And people suffered. Badly. Some emotionally and some physically and emotionally. Because the kundalini plexus was purely physical and without the heart there was no way to regulate it or keep it on the course of 'giving'. It would, as was the nature of all things existent, range from its highest potential of pleasure and bonding to its lowest potential of possessiveness and neediness. And people suffered.

For centuries people would suffer. Even after the kundalini had steadied and war and abuse had abated, people suffered emotionally as the heart had not awakened.

Niti just had to go through what she had to. They called it destiny in those days. He knew it was nothing more than the attribute of the soul to want to grow and keep adding energy till it could connect to the higher energies at their vibratory level through the human cerebral plexus. It was the journey.

The poor Love!

Four months since the Goa holiday and she felt like she needed another holiday! As an advertising professional, she enjoyed her job but being around celebrity and glamour and dealing with human moods and tantrums could take its toll on a person. And lately, it seemed to be every day! It was a challenge to stay relevant in the growing age of digital media anyway, and with goof-ups the size of the one today, they would sink for sure! So hard to get professional help today. Kids do a crash course in anything and think they're experts! Ugh! She was going to lose it one of these days if Anita, her boss, didn't do something about it soon.

And in the middle of all that stress, Salil called. He wanted to know if she could meet him for a coffee or a drink one of these days.

'Yes please!' She must have sounded desperate because he agreed to meet for a drink later that very evening.

'Great! I need some freshness and fun!'

'Bad day at work?'

'Bad days at work!'

'One large drink coming up! See you in a couple of hours.'

'See you.'

A lovely evening was had, as expected. They drank and laughed and he held her and comforted her. She remembered to ask how his divorce was going and he said his wife was creating problems but they should have it signed and dusted in the next month or so. She cuddled up to him in what she thought was a comforting manner, though it felt wonderful to her too. Drinks led to dinner, and they ate, though neither was really hungry. As the evening drew to a close, she said she'd get a cab, and he suggested he drop her off first and take the same cab home. She was OK with that.

And then he kissed her. It was delicious! There was nothing awkward about the first kiss. It thrilled her to know how natural it felt. She could get addicted to this stuff.

And then he kissed her again . . . and said good night.

She looked into his eyes for a while. They were excited, and he was definitely interested. He knew she lived alone. Was he waiting for her to ask him in? No. He'd said good night. He didn't want to be invited. He would have waited if he'd wanted her to offer.

She initiated one last kiss. He responded eagerly enough, but yet she said goodbye and stepped out of the cab.

So? What did that mean, do you think? She thought about it all that night and the next day and the next night. Should she call? Thank him for the other evening? Ask him if he's free this weekend?

She was still debating the diplomatic way of doing this when he called again. It was past eight, and she was home and warm and eating dinner.

'Are you at home?'

'Yes.'

'Do you have guests?'

'No.'

'Can I come over?'

Silence. 'Sure . . .' Silence. 'Is everything OK?'

'Can I tell you when I get there?'

'OK. Will see you in a few minutes then?'

'See you.'

In the end, she never did find out what had prompted that call because he didn't come over. He called again to say it wasn't fair to dump on her and he'd rather talk to her and distract himself. Things would fall into place anyway, he said. They always did. And anyway he was going to be travelling from the next day, so it wasn't that bad.

So they talked. A lot. It became a regular feature. One of them would call at the end of the day, and they would spend hours talking. About everything – politics, the state of the country, the marketing world, and the advertising world where life was going – everything was so much more interesting when discussing it with Salil. He travelled a lot, and the calls became a daily routine. They ate food whilst on the phone, they partied while talking to each other, and they even discussed movies and places as live updates.

It was exciting. She hadn't had this much fun in a long, long time. In fact, she couldn't remember when she'd let down her guard enough to have fun like this.

And then he said he would be back in Delhi for a while. They were both excited about actually meeting up again. It had been more than a month since the kiss. Niti wanted to know that thrill again.

And she got it.

Salil walked through her front door and kissed her. And then there was no talking for most of the night. Yes he was passionate and excited and he wanted her more than she had thought. Skolt could see the fire that swept Niti away. She was 'in love' with Salil. She was stimulated enough to be involved wholeheartedly this time, and for her usual level of involvement, she was already in above her head. But damn, it had to happen sometime, didn't it? Why not, Salil?

They had a torrid affair. He'd call out of the blue and she would always make sure she got home immediately, no matter where she was or what she was doing. They would have wild, crazy sex, lots and lots of talk and then he'd leave. He didn't want to ruin her reputation, he said. No promises. No plans on when to meet next. Their meetings always felt so short, and every time, after he left, she'd think of yet another zillion things she had wanted to talk to him about.

And then one day he told her his divorce was delayed and he had asked the company to send him to the head office in Singapore for a short stint. He needed a breather and he needed to give his wife some time to think.

Niti wasn't upset. It wasn't like they met every day. They had had three months together this time. More than she had expected. He had concocted work for the last two months to avoid travelling so he could be with her and she loved him even more for that. They had their phone calls. And they had emails. He said he would always be available on the mail. And it wasn't like he was going away tomorrow! He had put in a request. That was all. They'd deal with it when it happened, if it happened.

What really did happen, though, she was always a little foggy about. Salil kind of disappeared. The very next day after the conversation they'd had, he disappeared. Her calls and text messages went unanswered, as did the mails. Suddenly, he had disappeared.

Niti didn't panic. She thought he might have suddenly become very busy or gone on that trip. She went about her life like before but she kept trying to connect.

She thought about him all the time. She wondered about their status. She kept sending him the email communications though and she seriously thought about the length of time she would wait for him to respond. She didn't usually have to wait around so she truly had no idea what she would do but for now, she just kept doing what she was doing.

And she kept living her life the same as before – work, friends, and home. She had started a yoga class sometime back, but she had never been regular. Now she was. A friend had introduced her to meditation but she hadn't really taken to it. Too much stillness, she had thought. Now she gave it a shot. She started sitting in silence for a while every day, just to sort herself out. She'd ask questions into the silence and then get up. The answers never came but at least she knew what it was she wanted answers to.

What's going on?

Either he come in or cut him off.

I'm in a strange emotionless place. Get me out.

And then one day, he replied to an email! He'd been out of the country on a visit and been crazy busy. He was back for just this week and then would be gone for a month. Could

Niti come visit him at his place this time? He wouldn't have the time to come to her.

Suddenly, the day was brighter and there was a big, true smile on her face and excitement back in her life. Her meditation that morning was thank you, thank you, thank you! She hopped and skipped her way through work that day. She couldn't wait to see him again.

And then they were together.

She had so many questions to ask and lots to say. But, of course, none of that really happened. She was happy to go with his agenda. He looked genuinely tired and exhausted. They had comfort sex and then some crazy sex and then dinner. They talked and Salil explained how his wife was giving him trouble and he thought she was having him followed and his phone might be tapped so he had been taking things very, very easy. He was sorry and he looked it. And he looked tired. And then Salil just fell asleep sitting there talking to her! Just like that! That was how exhausted he must have been. Niti felt sorry for him. The poor guy. His life was obviously hectic, he hadn't been trying to fob her off. She kissed him good night and left.

She hadn't been asked to stay the night. He'd said something about his maid coming in early and that he thought she shouldn't be there then. It might cause trouble with his divorce. So Niti left.

And she never saw him again.

The first month she didn't worry about it too much. He had said he wouldn't be around. And he had said he was being cautious. She sent him the mails and messages anyway but less frequently and hesitatingly, chatting away about everything and anything.

Two months on and the mails became desperate. Where are you? Aren't you back yet? Will you please just reply this once and tell me that everything is OK. That's not too much to ask for, is it? But silence was all she got. She had a bad feeling about this.

She called his office and though the operator always said that she would put her through, for some reason, Niti was never put through. A couple of times of this brush-off and she stopped calling the office but she didn't stop trying to connect. The mails continued to go. She addressed formal official enquiry kind of mails to his office ID hoping he would respond in the guise of a business discussion.

It took her another month to realise that he was either dead or he consciously didn't want to get in touch with her. She had to accept that.

The heart break almost killed her. She stayed home from work for a week trying to understand what was happening. She wondered what had happened. She came up with a million scenarios for why he would have just left like that and another million scenarios about how he would come back to her, just like that. But nothing happened.

The attempts to connect became less frequent as did the messages.

She decided to get back to living. She decided to drum up some enthusiasm for life to start with.

The days got darker. Niti returned to wondering how long she was willing to wait for a reply. There was a kind of gloom over her. This time she was panicking. Something in her knew he wouldn't come back. She just knew.

He joy for life began to dry up. She became quiet and withdrawn. Only because she was waiting for him, she thought. She had to stop waiting. And she would. Very soon she would give up trying to connect and she would start getting over this whole episode. It hadn't been a love affair or anything like that. They had been a happenstance. A bad episode but then we all make mistakes and she could get it out of her system in no time once she'd decided to, she told herself. So she'd wait a little longer. Give him a chance to respond and if she didn't hear from him soon, she'd stop trying. Soon. Very soon.

That had been six months ago. Today, six months after the two months of trying, she was still trying. The mails went out weekly now but the text messages were over. Still silence from the other end.

Two months further down and she had lost her job and her joy in just about everything. Her friends thought she was depressed about her job and they were desperately sending out her resume to help her out. God bless them.

Oh yes! God! He was getting the brunt of it. All her dull calmness most of the day gave way to fiery temper in her meditations. They had become quite regular, by the way. She sat in silence only so she could fight with Him and vent. She begged her God and guides and angels. She said she wanted to know. That was all. She just wanted to know what the hell happened there. She was in a kind of limbo. She cried to them. She bargained. And she finally decided they were quite useless and she was going to get on with her life.

It wasn't like she and Salil had been a couple or had done things together that she should miss him. She'd just go out, party, make new friends and she'd be fine. Good as new.

With a big smile and renewed enthusiasm she started her life over. All the quotes and motivational talks all over the Internet said whatever one wants in life is what one should give. Set the intent and the universe will return it with interest, they said. Well, she wanted love.

She joined her friend's start-up that worked with farmers in India who were committing suicide because of climate change. She took a pay cut and was happy that she could do something to give back to society. She made new friends. She got back into the social scene.

But she never really healed again. She never became whole again. The men had no spark in their eyes and she felt no inclination to take any one of them up on their offer to get to know them better. She knew it would be a waste. They just weren't as interesting.

Niti didn't think of Salil consciously but she thought of him unconsciously all the time. He was always on her mind. She compared every man to him; she mentally thought about his reaction to her every act. She even wrote to him every month, even now, and gave him all her news. Yes! How stupid was that?

She loved him now in absentia much more than she had loved him when he was around.

Her meditations were getting intense. She was talking to the Big Guy all the time now. You're supposed to open a new door when you close the old one. Where's my door, Lord?

Things fall apart so new things will come into one's life. Where's the new, Lord?

Either get him back into my life or take away this yearning from my heart. Do something, Lord!

Ok, give me a sign. Tell me what you want me to do.

Kill me.

Nothing. Just the years passing by.

The deep anguish in her heart didn't subside. She tried harder to give love in the hope that the clichés were true and she would find her love.

Life went on silently by.

Niti projected a happy, bubbly person nonetheless. She had friends and was well loved. In her pretence to be happy, she actually laughed and lived. She became patron of an orphanage and found lots of children to share her love with. She almost got married once but then she decided against it.

And through it all, nobody knew that her heart had no place for anyone else. It already had someone and it had a big hole too. Everything else fell right through. She hadn't healed yet and she would never have been able to live her life where her heart wasn't involved. There was never going to be anyone else.

She gave up trying.

And yet she prayed for answers. She needed closure, she thought. Or maybe she needed to be loved. OK, she'd settle for being able to love, truly and with all her heart. But her heart remained silent.

By the time Niti's fiftieth birthday came around, she'd realised she was never going to heal and it would be best to plan her life around that fact. She still thought of Salil every day. An unknown number on her phone still had her thinking, maybe . . .

She spent her days sharing her life and expertise and the smile on her face with whoever came by her home and the orphanage. Her years of covering her pain had made her very aware of others and their feelings. Who knew how many were walking around with smiles on their faces and broken hearts?

The yoga and meditation had become a big part of her day. To be fair, she liked her solitude. She was happy alone. She would have loved company had it improved on her solitude but she refused to add anything to her life that took away the peace from her. Her meditations were more musings now. Of course, with the Big Guy for company!

Where did my prayers go, Lord, that you didn't reply?

How do people's dreams and desires come true?

They say we should be grateful to be alive and healthy, but how can I be grateful for what I don't want, Lord? This life lived like this is a burden. Take it back, Lord.

Did you also not ever love me, Lord? Why have you been silent all my life?

They say all prayers are answered and all wishes will eventually come true. Your time's up, Lord! Better hurry up with it . . .

But Salil never came. The call never came. And he never sent her a mail. She had no way of knowing what had happened to him or what had happened to them. There was no way of knowing. The company he had worked for had shown him as marketing manager for a couple of years and then he didn't feature on their employee list either.

Niti planned her old age with other single friends, some divorced and some widowed by then. Her parents had left her a nest-egg, and she had been wise most of her life. She could afford a good retirement.

It was an adventure in that time and age for all these oldies to be living together in a large community, enjoying their old age to the fullest.

People looked at Niti and cited her example. They said how happy and fulfilling life could be if you wanted it so, even if you were alone. What a lively old lady, they said. What fun to be free and spirited at this age, they agreed.

Little did they know that 90 per cent of the time this happy, lively old bird cried herself to sleep. Little did they know that the ache in her heart was such a permanent feature that she almost didn't feel it anymore. Till she did. And then it hurt again.

At the age of sixty-nine, Niti was outside, sitting under a beautiful bright sun, enjoying the weather. She remembered talking to her Big Guy. You failed me God, she said. And she could feel the old familiar ache in her heart. It was as piercing and real today as it had been thirty-five years ago. You failed me . . .

And suddenly, she was free! The ache was gone and the day was brighter than she could have imagined. She didn't have to look around to know she had left her body. She didn't look back even once. Without hesitation she marched on looking for the answers that had eluded her all her life.

The community hall was in a flurry that day. What a beautiful way to die, they said! Just like she had lived, she'd died. Quietly and peacefully. It had been a silent heart attack, they finally found out. What a lovely day it was! It suited Niti completely!

Yes. It would have had to be the heart, thought Skolt. The poor organ had taken such a beating it was bound to give up, he thought wryly. It had been a sad life. However inspiring on the surface, the anguish of living lovelessly had taken its toll forever. Sad, by human judgement. The soul though must have happily laughed the life through. It could feel the heart plexus opening after all. Happiness does not create opportunity to stretch ones limits. The emotion of pain, in humans, is what tests our endurance and thus causes surplus energy generation.

And the heart ached because it was trying very hard to respond to the messages sent by the heart plexus, but the intellect and social indoctrinations didn't allow for expression. And the burden of stifled feelings caused strain on the plexus region.

Feelings were real, and they had energy. They could damage organs far more than physical causes could.

He was mighty sure that Salil had died of a heart attack too in that life time. Whether he had even remembered Niti past the year they had been together or not, the signals her heart had been sending out all those years had definitely reached his heart plexus. Salil's energies would have read the messages and wanted to respond but his intellect couldn't pick up the messages and that would create hurdles and obstacles. The heart plexus cares nothing for your social laws and limitations. It can only respond with a high frequency that may translate as love or compassion or sympathy or friendship or companionship. All the heart trouble Salil must have had over the years was nothing more than energies struggling for expression.

Skolt sat in silence wondering why Niti's life was troubling him so much. He could still feel her anguish and helplessness. Those were non-existent emotions in the world today but he could relate. It was almost like he was reliving that life. Why?

My Word: 2016 CE
                                              India

This being a physical era, most relationships require physical expression. There are very few souls who form a relationship that vibrates at a frequency higher than the kundalini plexus and they don't have the physical weighing down on them. But all relationships, All relationships, will eventually move past the physical and rise with time. They will be required to and will manifest different forms of soul expression.

It is sad that people in this era cannot see that. They assume that when the physical is over in a relationship, the relationship is over. They struggle so hard to bring back the physical. They work ON the physical level to re-liven the physical expression of their relationship, little realising that allowing the energy to grow and expressing your soul in other ways will keep the physical alive albeit in lesser focus. The more we focus on a lesser energy than the level the soul is vibrating at the more we get stuck in the energy web. Relationships are meant to help us grow and not bring us down.

All physical ailments, the so-called lifestyle diseases, the mental disorders, the new diseases being discovered every day by medical scientists are nothing more than symptoms of energy suppression. They are not the problem per se. Suppression of your soul energy is.

Every day there is a new scare. Elbows are dry due to lack of vitamin 0. Lips are cracked? You're suffering from xyz. Grey hair? Let's tweak your genes. Brittle cuticles? You're going to die.

Come on!

But yes, being in sync with your energy level and being able to live to express that level is the only way to a healthy and productive life.

Love and Happiness ☺

Chapter 4

'Yes yes, Hoyt! I'm here, right here! What's the excitement about?'

'I'm sending you a document. Tell us what you think.'

The Book of Intelligence
31 jan 14016

Intellect and Its Progression

This isn't a theory or a philosophy. This is the interpretation of old scriptures and ancient books that have carried the information in their depths forever but have been ignored for the longest time and when studied, have for the larger part, been misinterpreted. The last written text was approx. 24,000 years ago but we have found reference of this teaching in oral context going back almost 36,000–48,000 years ago from this year of 14016.

These scriptures were last correctly interpreted when the Asian Subcontinent was a seeker's land, approx. 24,000 years ago. Where intelligence was at its peak and everybody was a curious scientist. Fear of God and religion had not entered the lives of people. Population was scanty and man lived in harmony with nature and the universe, thus making it easier for him to access higher truths and experiment with

1

them till he could bring them down to the level of human consciousness. This was the last time man had brain capacity of close to 100 per cent. Ever since, his capacity as well as his intellect had only gradually reduced, coming down to less than 25 per cent. These studies were grossly misunderstood and misinterpreted during those times. Brain capacity slowly began its ascend and today 12,000 years after that lowest point we are back to 100 per cent brain capacity and thus it is believed that the current interpretations are correct and true.

How you ask?

A study of the Akashic Records has revealed that the intellect and its growth is related to the movement of the planet towards and away from its magnetic centre, 'Eye of Gaia'.

As we are aware, Earth, in its movements of rotation and revolution, is also part of the galaxy's movement around its twin Sun. This brings the planet in close proximity to its magnetic centre, 'Eye of Gaia'. The journey to the closest point of contact takes approximately 12,000 years and the time to move from there to the furthest point takes another 12,000 years. This cycle is called 'Gaia Din' from the Sanskrit word-meaning day.

It was so far assumed that the journey of 24,000 years had no greater significance on the earth than to help calculate the age of the universe, man's evolution and journey and the life times of certain extinct phenomena. The larger time lines helped accurately chronicle timelines.

2

The Book of Intelligence
31 jan 14016

With further research, it seems, the 'Eye of Gaia' has more significance than that!

The Yugas,

The ancient texts talk about the yugas. That was a time when the wise men and sages wrote in their language as they interpreted the truths. Their words and nomenclature are their own creations but I shall use them, as it will be easier to speak to you in their language.

There are four yugas in all. A great sage, Manu, spoke about the division of Eternal Time and gave each segment a name. He named them Kali Yuga, Dwapara Yuga, Treta Yuga, and Satya Yuga. These names have lasted the centuries and are still used to explain this concept. The concept isn't new and it doesn't need new names to be explained. And once understanding is got, the names will not matter again. Time will, in your mind, again be just time.

A little bit of astronomy, astrology, and mathematics is now called for . . .

* refer to image on p 66

We learn from astronomy that moons revolve around their planets and planets spin on their axis and along with their moons, revolve around their sun.

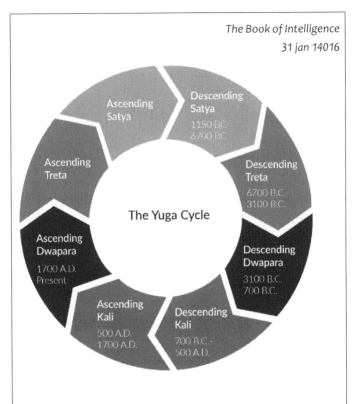

Oriental astronomy had something else to add. It says that the sun, with its planets and their moons, takes another star as its dual and revolves around it. The spinning of the moon takes twenty-four hours, the revolution of the earth takes twelve months, and the revolution of the sun takes – wait for it – 24,000 years! This is a celestial phenomenon that causes the backward movement of equinoctial points around the zodiac. These are facts that can be verified from any astronomical data.

4

The Book of Intelligence
31 jan 14016

Just like we have day/night due to rotation of the Earth and summer/winter because of revolution, similarly, our galaxy revolves around a magnetic point which was termed by the yogis, thousands of years ago as 'Brahma ki aankh' or 'eye of Brahma'.

(That's a magnetic point light years away. Don't worry that our scientists haven't discovered it as yet, the telescope itself was discovered merely 600 years ago. They haven't had enough time as yet!)

This revolution of the solar system around the 'magnetic eye' also causes certain changes to occur on, and in, life on earth.

Just like rotation causes tide movements, and revolution causes seasons, similarly, the magnetic point affects the finer vibrations that exist on earth – like mind-waves and their movements.

Detailed Explanation:

When our galaxy and subsequently, our planet, are furthest away from this magnetic point, it creates an atmosphere on earth that is thick, dense, and heavy. The heavy density and thickness of atmosphere does not cause obstacles for man's physical form, but it affects man's finer vibrations like thought waves, mind-energy, and heart waves. These are very fine, high vibrations, and they cannot travel smoothly in the thickness of the plane they

5

move in. Consequently, man is almost like a 'cave man'. With low heart waves, he 'feels' less – less compassion, less loving, more selfish, more violent. With low thought waves there is lack of emotional understanding, telepathy is non-existent. Understanding of God and matters that cannot be seen or experienced by the physical senses, cannot be had without mind energy. So man is largely 'unrefined'.

This was termed as 'Kalyuga'.

When the sun gets to the point where it is furthest from this grand magnetic centre, an event that takes place when the Autumnal Equinox is on the first point of Libra, the mental capacity of man comes to such a reduced state that man cannot grasp anything beyond the gross material creation.

This is Kalyuga, the Dark Ages. The lowest point on the cycle and in mankind's evolution.

These are the Dark Ages. There is fear for the continuance of humanity as it stands, for man will kill man for his own selfish needs in times like these. Dark or kaala as it is called in Sanskrit – which gives us the 'Kali Yuga' or Kalyuga. This yuga lasts for a 1,000 years with 100 years as a 'sandhi' period at the start and end. ('sandhi' or merging, in Sanskrit) which is a total of 1,200 years.

Summary:

In the ascending cycle, the time of 1,200 years when the sun passes through 1/20th of its orbit furthest away from the magnetic point was called the Kali Yuga. Mental capacity is then in its first stage and only a quarter developed. The

The Book of Intelligence
31 jan 14016

human intellect cannot comprehend anything beyond the gross material of the external world.

As we get moving towards the magnetic point, the atmosphere begins to lose its density. Slightly and slowly it gets a little rarefied – which means heart waves begin to travel and they are able to touch the other being and man begins to feel. He feels for others, he feels for animals, for the environment, he worries about the future. He feels another's pain and happiness. Understanding of God and the universe and subtle things that one can sense but which are not tangible also find place in his understandings. He's still a bit of a cave man in the beginning . . . he fights. But now – he fights for peace, for love. He craves peace and calm now to get on with all the things he has to understand.

The understanding of electricity becomes apparent. Electricity will take over his life. There are four kinds of electricity in all that man will discover in the course of this yuga. He will use them in every possible way.

And this creates His second yuga or Dwapara Yuga, where dwapara comes from the Sanskrit word 'dwi' or two. A yuga of oncoming peace and ease. This yuga lasts 2,000 years with 200 years sandhi on either side. A total of 2,400 years.

Summary:

The period of 2,400 years during which the sun passes through the 2/20th part of its orbit was called the Dwapara Yuga. Mental capacity is then in the second stage of development, and man can comprehend the fine matters or electricity and their attributes which are the creating principles of the external world.

Onwards to the third yuga or Treta Yuga. The air or atmosphere is even more rarefied. The physical body continues as always but it now follows the dictates of the heart and the higher understanding of the mind. Most of civilisation will have the understanding of what we call 'spirituality' these days. It will be common place rather than hard-to-understand. That will be the reality then. Understanding of magnetism will be profound. In fact, cutting up bodies and sophisticated operations as you see them today will be considered gross! All will be healed through magnetic therapy. All the sci-fi stuff that you can imagine, that can happen magnetically, will happen. It will be a time of utmost peace. Telepathy and mental understanding will be the way of communication. No more women from Venus and men from Mars. There will be bigger things to write and work on, than human difficulties in relationships because human difficulties will no more be the dominant factor in lives. Relationships will be deeper and be more for growth of the individual than for dependency or continuation of the species.

That is the Treta Yuga. Going closer to the magnetic centre and helping man use almost 80 per cent of his brain power at this point. This yuga lasts 3,000 years with 300 years of sandhi on both sides. That is 3,600 years.

The Book of Intelligence
31 Jan 14016

Summary:

The period of 3,600 years during which the sun is in the 3/20th part of its journey was called the Treta Yuga. Mental capacities are then in the third stage and human intellect becomes able to comprehend the divine magnetism, the source of all electrical forces on which the creation depends for its existence.

At the highest point is Satya Yuga; when the sun in its revolution round its dual comes to the place closest to the grand magnetic centre, an event that takes place when the autumnal equinox comes to the first point of Aries. Mental capacity is so highly developed that man can easily comprehend all, even the mysteries of Spirit.

And this, of course, is Satya Yuga, the time of heaven on earth. Everything exactly as you dream about now. Beauty, understanding, love . . . all at exemplary levels. Perfection as we can only imagine. This is when man uses a 100 per cent of his brain power. Can you imagine what he can do with that? He is able to understand and relate to all that there is, in the material world and the 'spiritual'. He enjoys perfect peace and calm. Crystal therapy is the panacea for all human ailments then because vibes from crystals travel freely and smoothly in that state. In the other yugas also, crystal emits its energy but it can reach and be absorbed only by those who vibrate at a higher frequency. The others only receive fractured benefits. But in the Satya Yuga, crystal will be the way of treatment.

9

This yuga lasts the longest, four thousand years with 400 years of sandhi both sides. A total of 4,800 years. And a double Satya Yuga means a long and peaceful time on earth. (See the diagram.)

Summary:

The period of 4,800 years during which the sun passes through the 4/20th part of its orbit was called the Satya Yuga. Mental abilities are in the fourth stage and completes their full development. Human intellect can now comprehend all, even God and Spirit and all beyond this physical world.

And then you would be as close to the magnetic centre as you can get. The half-cycle lasts for a total of 12,000 years. As the galaxy rolls back the reverse continues to happen. As man kills the ego and finds peace and happiness and oneness, so does he find saturation in that peace and love. He becomes complacent, and the ego takes over again and then begins his downfall into the Dark Ages again – which is another 12,000 years, after which man will become his lowest self again.

Each of these periods of 12,000 years brings a complete change, both externally in the material world, and internally in the intellectual or electric world, and is called one 'electric couple'. Thus, in a period of 24,000 years, the sun completes the revolution around its dual and finishes one electric cycle consisting of 12,000 years in an ascending arc and 12,000 years in a descending arc.

10

Necessary to mention that in every yuga, there are people who will be exceptions to the rule. There will be some who look like they never left the Dark Ages, and there will always be some who have defeated the material restrictions of the yugas and gone past.

The original text:

This detailed study was first described by Manu, a great rishi of the 'Satya Yuga'. He said:

चत्वार्याहुः सहस्राणि वर्षाणान्तु कृतं युगम् ।
तस्य तावच्छती सन्ध्यां सन्ध्यांश्च तथाविधः ॥
इतरेषु ससन्ध्येषु ससन्ध्यांशेषु च त्रिषु ।
एकापायेन वर्तन्ते सहस्राणि शतानि च ॥
यदेतत् परिसंख्यातमादावेव चतुर्युगम् ।
एतद् द्वादशसाहस्रं देवानां युगमुच्यते ॥
दैविकानां युगानान्तु सहस्रं परिसंख्यया ।
ब्राह्ममेकमहर्ज्ञेयं तावती रात्रिरेव च ॥

(The original Sanskrit verse)1
Meaning:

Four thousands of years, they say, is the Satya Yuga. Its morning twilight has just as many hundreds and its period of evening dusk is of the same length (i.e., 400 + 4,000 + 400 = 4,800). In the other three ages, with their morning and evening twilights, the thousands and hundreds decrease by

---

1   From The Laws of Manu pg. 11

---

one (i.e., 300 = 3,000 = 300 = 3,600; etc). That fourfold cycle comprising 12,000 years is an Age of the Go)

At the time when intelligence was at its peak, man was able to comprehend the mysteries of the universe and all that he set his mind to opened up and revealed itself to him. Thus, the advancements to science made in that era will always be an absolute truth, and everything else can only at best be speculation.

12

'Hmmmm . . .,' Skolt knew they had found the seed-thought behind the theory, 'makes a lot of sense.' He was still thoughtful. 'OK. Bring in the references, the lead-up, and the support information. Great going, team! I think we've almost closed this!'

He had thought it would take them longer than this, but it was great how fast they had figured this out! This was after all a high-energy research group, and while each person in this day and age worked for his energy growth, it naturally worked out that each assisted the other for their own inner growth. The Akashic Records, of course, were an added assistance for speedy references and research.

He had created this group to help him refurbish all the information that ever existed and bring it up to date. He was supposed to clear out data that had collected but was not required, like in the age of Google, when everything was stored in the 'cloud', there was a lot of electronic data stored that was completely not correct or not valid for human growth. It was the era of learning and people went through a lot of trial and error, which was all recorded in the Akashic Records. It was his life's work to clean up that information. Though one can never completely wipe out information from the Records, one can keep bringing up relevant information to the point where the irrelevant matter got deeply buried. So hopefully in the next round of yugas when man sat in contemplation and came up with solutions to problems that they believed they had 'dreamed' up but had actually accessed from the Records, it would most probably be the right or most relevant solutions.

He was excited and he immediately settled into the sheetla mode to communicate with the higher energies. He needed to know if he was on the right track and what he was supposed to do now. And he wanted to know why Niti was possessing him so.

You want to know what to do now? Seriously?

He could sense the exaggerated incredulousness!

He, who had been defying the Energies ever since his Niti lifetime, had always been one to push the envelope. He had always wondered what would happen if . . .

And the more he pushed, the more he realised that there was no limit. You were free to learn, to create, and to become whatever your energies are leading you to. But yes, the energies are limiting forces. If your energy level is not sufficiently raised to connect with its source unconsciously, then no matter how hard you try, it won't happen consciously. One has to raise the energy level and all else will follow, naturally.

For a few centuries and through a certain era, it was believed that time is linear and humans are living many lifetimes simultaneously. There was also talk of visiting one's childhood or a previous lifetime or a future lifetime.

Having come well ahead of that era and looking back, Skolt could see how that misconception could arise. After all people had no connection with the Akashic Records then. In deep contemplation or what they called 'meditative state', people unconsciously and instinctively stepped into the Records and they could see their past lives. Vividly and as close to 'real' as possible, they were able to view events. This didn't mean that they were visiting that life again. Once you have passed an energy level, there's no going back.

How he wished it were possible to go back though. He'd visit Niti and show her how much love she had actually amassed in that lifetime and help her see the real purpose of her feelings for Salil. Maybe the anguish would be less if the journey was clearer.

But with less anguish, the purpose would not be met! More the tragedy! That to be aware of love and faith and your ability to deal with pain is the very journey that takes your energy to levels beyond compare. Of course, to be happy finally and find wish fulfilment is the game plan, usually. He'd love to know how Niti had been the exception to the rule. There are usually no exceptions in Universal Laws. They work exactly the same for everyone.

Which would mean? That wish fulfilment is yet to occur? Which means . . . ! Really? There was more to his story? He might just reunite with that soul energy that had been niggling away at him for lifetimes? That would be something!

He could feel his sense of excitement reach fever pitch. Salil could be born male or female in this lifetime and it wouldn't matter. The soul energy connection that his energies were craving had been waiting a long time. There was something in that connection that was going to complete his journey. He just knew it. He wasn't coming onto this planet, time and again, just to share his knowledge with other souls. No. He had unfinished business here. Once that was done, he was free to merge with the higher energies. He would be free.

Skolt opened his eyes with renewed purpose. This sheetla had been informative!

And that was always how sheetla worked. Unknowingly to you, it answered all your questions.

Chapter 5

'Well, it's simple enough to understand. That the magnetic centre not only marks the cycle of 12,000–24,000 years but also causes some changes on the earth's environment that enables our brain capabilities to go from below 25 per cent to almost 100 per cent. That makes sense.' Isabella was crisp and studious-sounding in her summary of the paper Skolt had just shared with them.

'And this would explain why Darwin could not grasp the soul story of evolution too,' continued Holly. 'They simply could not understand it as their minds were in a physical plane, as you said, Skolt.'

'Yes. The understanding that energies evolve through a physical plane mode and then emotional followed by mental and finally spiritual modes has been well documented and we've seen it happening repeatedly in cycles. What causes it though, was not documented. At least not recently. The fact that it exists in the Records is proof that it was known and documented but not in the data of this cycle of "Gaia Din".'

'The cause is the "Gaia Din". The journey to and from the "Eye of Gaia"?'

'Yes.'

'And what is the significance of this knowledge?' Danube, the thinker was at it again.

'Why don't you tell me that? Think about it and let me know how this knowledge will benefit human growth.'

'Well, since we already know that we are in the first phase of the descending Satya Yuga, does that mean that intelligence will begin to decrease from now? Which means that every successive generation will be less intelligent?'

'Yes, I guess.'

'That's a scary thought!'

'Intelligence,' Skolt clarified, 'is the ability to understand, retain and use knowledge as and when needed. Wisdom on the other hand is to be able to filter knowledge through the heart plexus and sense what to use, when to use and how to use knowledge for the growth and betterment of all. When I say "all", I mean "life and environment of the planet". Animate and inanimate. So it will be wisdom that will be the first casualty in the descending process. And then will be the intelligence to rightly understand and interpret knowledge that will go. In extreme cases and areas of the planet, knowledge of language and basics has also been known to be lost.'

'The Dark Ages!'

'Yes.'

'And then it picks up again?'

'Fortunately yes,' nodded Skolt, 'language interpretation of knowledge takes place instinctively. And as intellectual competence grows, the ability to use knowledge and discover new phenomenon begins to occur.'

'So does every cycle show new discoveries for man and life?'

'Sorry, I should have said "rediscover". It's an endless cycle of rediscovery! Man will forget electricity and aerodynamics in another few thousand years and then rediscover it 12,000 years later. Our awareness of energy balance and our connection with the higher energies and soul energy is so natural to us, but humans will lose touch with it very soon. They will be unable to grasp this communication for thousands of years to come and will begin the search again at the start of the ascending Satya Yuga which is almost 15,000 years away!'

'But once the soul has achieved a particular energy level, it cannot regress. How, then, can it forget?'

'The souls that have achieved enough energy to merge with the higher energies will leave their earth connections and move to different planes as the yuga begins to change but other souls that have been waiting for the right energy level, like souls that had incomplete work in the last Dwapara or Treta Yuga will come back in this one to finish their journey.'

'But they may not finish their journey and the yuga might finish?'

'Yes, but energy only rises. So these souls will be of a higher energy level when the lower yuga arrives and the higher energy souls become guides and masters to the lesser energy beings. They come as prophets and gurus. You will find mention of a number of prophets and gurus in the descending yugas, from the second half of Descending Treta Yuga (DTY) to the first half of Ascending Treta Yuga (ATY) and especially around the Kalyuga. The guides and masters and gurus would assist souls to higher energy levels but because of lack of understanding in the lower energy souls they would treat the guide souls as The Source. They called them "God". And treated them as such. People created religions around these guide souls and their teachings.'

'Is that why there were a number of religions in the ancient world?'

'Yes. Many religions as obviously there must have been many advanced souls. As understanding grew, every guru or master's teachings were not made into religions any more but the status remained the same. The master was "God".'

'Is that the main purpose of these advanced souls? To be teachers?'

'It is very difficult to structure that, Isabella. Advanced souls, but naturally, leave their learnings in the world. It is a necessity of life itself and the nature of soul energy that it leaves an imprint in the material world. That imprint almost always moves evolution along. Whether it is a parent's teachings to the child or a teacher's guidance, these are all imprints of advanced soul. The problem arises when ignorance and need creates a larger-than-real ego. That is when humans, for the sake of ego gratification, like – name, fame, glory and money – indulge in false belief. They believe they have teachings and guidance to share but in reality they merely have knowledge and are still firmly living in the kundalini plexus. Knowledge that has not travelled through the heart plexus and the cerebral plexus does not carry enough wisdom to be shared.'

'But the general public would not have understood that wisdom anyway. They did not have a well developed heart plexus themselves!'

'That is true, but – the truth always resonates. So, even if people could not completely understand and use the wisdom of the wise, they could sense the truth and aspire to it. Of course, there was a time when the heart plexus was opened for some, and at one time for almost all, when further complications occurred . . .'

'Like . . . ?'

'Well, people were plain emotional. Or sentimental, shall we say. They lived out of the heart alone. The physical plane was, of course, a given but the heart was the focus. It was a fuzzy, happy, dreamy, unreal world they believed in and convinced the yet-to-awaken souls to believe in! People actually believed that to imagine love existed and to give and to believe one was happy and grateful and enlightened would cause it to happen!' Skolt smiled at the images that brought up. He had encountered such souls in his lifetime as Niti and again in his lifetime as Kalki. They had been happy souls though, he had to admit! Lost, but happy. And that was a big commodity in those days. The purpose of the soul, though, is not to be happy, contrary to the popular belief of the ancient humans. Its sole purpose is to grow and collect enough energy to merge with the cosmic energy. Single point agenda. And that final merging level of growth cannot happen without activating the cerebral plexus.

'Enlightened?'

'Oh yes! But that's another story for another time!'

Skolt would have liked to rest under the trees for a while. He did not need much sleep as his deep sheetla kept him rejuvenated. And a moment's rest in the natural forests and gardens around him accomplished the rest. They could refresh anytime.

As was the way of the world in this era, people lived in environmentally friendly homes and kept the environment mostly natural. There were no cars and personal transport vehicles. There were no roads and streets either. Natural growth existed everywhere and paths were made for pedestrians and non-motorised vehicles. Natural paths – of mud and regular footfall – was all one saw even in busy cities.

People were connected to each other telepathically and souls were always so close that needless physical movement was not required. Proximity, when required, was accomplished either by non-motorised vehicles or public natural-gas equipped vehicles. The higher souls simply transported themselves to their required destinations. People could be found resting under trees and bushes everywhere. Singles, couples or in groups – active and animated or in sheetla . . . men and women were always found in the open. Their need to commune with nature and the higher energies drove them into the open all the time.

But as Skolt made to settle himself under a canopy of trees, he felt Hoyt seeking entry. He moved in and out of Skolt's consciousness as was typical of Hoyt's restless energy!

'Yes, Hoyt. Yes!' That was Skolt's customary greeting for Hoyt.

'We have an explanatory document we'd like you to read and reference. Sending . . .'

The Book of Intelligence
31 Jan 14016

Proof of Ascension of Limited Intelligence:

Reference to the yugas and their structure are found right through history. The right interpretation was available till the DDY (Descending Dwapara Yuga), after which the information was lost and though awareness of yugas remained, the timelines and purpose of yugas was wiped out. Man believed that the Kalyuga or the Dark Ages would last for many hundred thousand years! And the ignorant ancient humans lived in that belief for years.

It is noticed that, even though some advanced souls had in the past, rightly interpreted the yuga theory, the general human race was unwilling to accept it. There were several reasons, as we understand it:

1. Spiritual understanding was non-existent in the descending and ascending Kalyuga and for part of the ascending Dwapara Yuga. So the science that related to spirituality was denied and unaccepted.

13

It is to be noted that material science was thriving at the very same time. Concepts such as gravity and atomic energy and astronomy were being widely understood, while finer concepts like that of spiritual science were rejected.

2. It was an era of religions during the DKY, AKY, and ADY. Spiritual science originated from the Indian subcontinent and was considered a concept of Hinduism, the religion followed by the majority of humans living there. 'Yoga', or at least their version of it, was revived and taught during the A.D.Y. but it was still considered 'Hinduism' and therefore not unanimously accepted by followers of other religions. The other scientific concepts, like gravity, magnetism etc., though originating in lands that followed 'Christianity' were not considered religious and therefore unanimously accepted.

This is in keeping with our understanding that during the Kalyuga and the Dwapara Yuga human intellect was incapable of understanding concepts beyond the physical reality. Even though these concepts were brought into human awareness, only very few benefitted from this knowledge.

There are writings of Swami Sri Yukteshwar Giri and of Sri Sri Paramahansa Yogananda that make reference to the yuga theory and one book in particular that discusses it in detail. And though these books were widely read, they were not understood or accepted enough for people to

14

believe the yugas were as relevant to human existence as was weather and day/night and neither did they understand the timeline to correct their belief of Kalyuga.

Due to some past mistakes in the almanacs, the Dwapara Yuga was initially recorded as Kali Yuga.

Swami Sri Yukteshwar Giriji explains how this mistake occurred.

After Mahabharata war, Pandavas (Dharmaraja and his four brothers)*2 along with other wise men retired to the Himalayas. Dharmaraja's grandson Raja Parikshit took the throne. No one in his court had the understanding of the yugas.

First mistake: When the Dwapara ended after 2,400 years in 701 BC, no one dared to change to Kali Yuga due to lack of understanding. Dwapara Yuga continued even though it actually ended.

Second mistake: In between someone changed the yuga to Kali Yuga and started counting the years from the previous Dwapara. So AD 499 became Kali Yuga 3,600 (this included Dwapara 2,400 + Kali Yuga 1,200)

Third mistake: After AD 499, with the start of Ascending Kali Yuga, intellectual understanding started to develop. So some wise men of the time understood that there was some mistake in this calculation. However their understanding did not develop to the extent of correcting the mistake. So

15

instead of correcting the mistake, they assumed that the ancestors must be right in continuing Kali Yuga and tried to fit the numbers into this argument. They fancied that though Kali Yuga is supposed to have only 1,200 years, these years are not ordinary years, they are daiva (divine, or age of Gods) years consisting of twelve daiva months of thirty daiva days each, with each day equal to one earth year.

So 1,200 years of Kali Yuga counted as daiva years = 1,200 × 12 × 30 earth years = 432,000 years

According to this wrong calculation, we have completed 5,115 years (in 2015, when the first correction was published) of Kali Yuga and still 432,000 – 5,115 = 426,885 years of Kali Yuga are left!

In Swami Yukteshwar's words, a dark prospect, fortunately not true!

Proof of Progression of Yuga

Ascending Dwapara Yuga (A.D.Y.) started in AD 1699. For reference, the year 2015 is 315 years into Ascending Dwapara Yuga. The following table shows the time line.

| | | *The Book of Intelligence* |
		31 jan 14016
AD 499	Sun reached farthest point from the grand centre in its cycle. This is the darkest period of the total cycle of 24,000 years.	
AD 499	Sun started moving in reverse and the ascending Kali Yuga started	During the next 1,100 years of Kali Yuga, the human intellect remained ignorant and no comprehension of the fine matters of creation. In AD 1599 the transition time from Kali Yuga started and men began to observe the fine matters (pancha tanmatraas) or the attributes of electricity. Political peace also started getting established. AD 1600 William Gilbert discovered magnetic forces. AD 1609 – Kepler discovered laws of astronomy, Galileo invented telescope. AD 1621 – Drebbal of Holland invented microscope. AD 1670 – Newton discovered law of gravitation

		The Book of Intelligence *31 jan 14016*
AD 1699	Ascending Dwapara Yuga (sandhi period) started	AD 1700 – Thomas Savery made use of a steam engine in raising water.
		AD 1720 – Stephen Gray discovered action of electricity on human body.
		AD 1873 – James Maxwell – theory of electro magnetism
		AD 1895 – Rontgen – discovers X rays
		AD 1896 – Henri BecQuerel discovers radioactivity
		AD 1897 – JJ Thomson discovers electron in cathode rays
1899	200 years transition time of Ascending Dwapara ended and Dwapara proper started.	AD 1900 – Max Plank – Law of black body radiation
		AD 1915 – Albert Einstein Theory of general relativity
		AD 1925 – Schrodinger equation (Quantum mechanics)
		AD 1927 – Heisenburg principle (Quantum mechanics)
		AD 1947 – First transistor invented by Shockley, Bardeen and Brattain
		AD 1971 – Microprocessor invented by Faggin, Hoff, and Mazor.
		AD 1979 Cell phone

'Hmmmm . . .' Skolt was thoughtful.

'What?' Hoyt sounded distracted.

'Why is this information important for human beings? Why do they need to know?' He remembered Danube's question.

'Why? What do you mean why?'

'Unhunh. Why?'

'Why do people need to know about weather? They'd just pack themselves up when they feel cold and strip when they're warm. Or carry an umbrella when it looks like rain. Why did man have to study weather and create meteorological departments?'

'Oh. That's why?'

'I mean why do you need to know "why" we have day and night! We just do. Deal with it. Sleep when you want. Or don't. Whatever.'

Skolt almost laughed out loud at Hoyt's indignation. He was offended because he had been asked to defend research and information collection? He, Skolt, could think of a million reasons for 'why' we need to know things and he was sure when Hoyt calmed down there would be a barrage of list as to 'why' we need research.

'What do you mean "why"? And why do you need to know "why"?'

'Skolt, do you want us to do a relevance study?' Kiera interjected softly.

'Yes please Kiera.' Skolt replied equally softly and telepathically, and silently, blocked out his senior researchers.

Almost done, he thought. The book of intelligence is almost complete.

As with all documents and scriptures written during a Satya Yuga period, too much detail is not given. Thoughts or directives are clipped, to-the-point and almost terse. It is understood that these facts will be subject to interpretation over the coming centuries and each generation will interpret them as per their social and intellectual level. These documents needed to be researched and deeply contemplated upon to be comprehended completely. They weren't for the lazy intellectual or the language savvy at all. They were for the dedicated learner. Therefore they were open-ended documents.

The last Satya Yuga that took place in the Indian subcontinent had scripts like the Upanishads and the Yoga Sutras by Patanjali.

Sutras were terse expressions that were mostly unintelligible and allowed for numerous interpretations. This is the method in which many very old scriptures were written by the wise to protect them from loose interpretations and keep from diluting the gravity of the information they carried. The sutras can almost never be understood without commentary and they almost always carry the flavour and bias of the interpreter and the state of society at the time of interpretation. Therefore the scriptures are translated again and again at different time lags to keep them updated with the times.

The Sutras by Patanjali were interpreted right through the A.D.Y. and into the A.T.Y. by which time they had been accepted as a way of life and even though all humans did not live by his yogic ways, enough followed the scriptures to be able to help evolution of soul energy along. His writings eventually went back into obscurity by late ATY but by then they had done their job and pulled humanity through an entire yuga into the next.

The Upanishad's too, were concepts of life and living, written as cryptic questions and answers. Despite their being close to thirteen volumes of the Upanishads, they don't bear their author's names. The names of the researchers were never important. Glory, name and fame don't belong to the Satya Yuga. All energy is one. The knowledge needs to carry on – that is all that matters.

This Satya Yuga has seen life in the central plane, what was at one time the Mediterranean region. The Indian subcontinent is mostly water and the other continents were left to grow naturally so as to bring back the balance between nature and environment and human/animal life.

Not many souls have the high energy to be born in this yuga and population is low. Though the souls are in no hurry to go back either and their life span is long!

Would Salil be here now? Had his energies reached the level of a Satya Yuga birth? Must be, else he wouldn't be feeling these strong vibes at this time. Salil was close. He could sense it. Just born maybe? The thought suddenly struck him. No, please – he hoped not. He didn't have time for a child in this lifetime.

My Word: 2016 CE
                                                India

The reason to know that you are emerging from the Kali Yuga that has lasted 2,400 years, even longer than your current calendar, is to be aware that all that you believe today, or have been taught or have come to accept as the way of life has been seeped in 100s of years of limited understanding. It has come from a place of fear. Fear has been the result and the cause of the Dark Ages and all that you live by today was taught by your ancestors out of their lack of understanding of reality, which translated into fear.

But today, you stand in a different yuga. You have passed the sandhi years of the Dwapara Yuga and are in the Dwapara Yuga proper. The very atmosphere is different. Your understanding is way beyond what the generations before you could dream of understanding. You come from a place of love.

Forget what you were told. If you are looking to give up fear then nothing can hold you back but fear itself. Drop it now. You belong to this era. You can accept it right now, this very minute and you will feel the energy rise in you. Don't hold the children back. Don't instil fear in them.

Love. Love is what this yuga is all about. You have 2,400 years to master it, though it would be best if you figured it out now. This instant. You are a child of this current universe. Live in this present yuga. Rejoice in it.

The yugas exist. This is a Universal Truth.

The yuga you are in is a piece of destiny beyond your control. But the reason you belong to this yuga and not the one before this can only be because you were destined for Love and greater Understanding. Don't let the Old Ways influence you. We are still at a tender point in our entry into these higher energy zones. More the people who believe, more will be the strength in the energies.

Don't look for proof outside of yourself. Don't look for signs and symbols from the universe. You are connected to the whole universe from inside of you. Go within. Find the truth from inside you. Believe it. And then ... live your truth. Knowing that there is nothing to fear and nothing can stop you growing as long as you choose love and inner understanding to do it. All else will fail in this yuga. But with Love – You Just Cannot Fail!

Signs and symbols were required for the time when understanding was limited but today – now – exercise your growing understanding. Exercise your Inner Wisdom. That's the only way to make it grow.

Love and Happiness ☺

Skolt opened his eyes, immediately alert. The message he had just received in sheetla seemed to be for his Niti lifetime. Was it for him? Had he chosen love over fear? Had he, unknowingly, done the right thing at the right place in the right yuga? All he could remember doing was living. Trying to make every moment count despite the constant ache in his heart. He could remember nothing more important than that in that lifetime.

Though in hindsight, it was obvious that that was all that was ever required. To live life right now, right here, to the fullest. There was no point affirming happiness and love and abundance when one was experiencing pain and heart break and strife. That would be equivalent to lying to oneself and the soul is aware of the experience being lived, it cannot lie. Best is to live with and through whatever situation one has in life because that very situation and that very experience is what is required for one's own growth. Denying it is never, never going to work. But also – don't judge it.

The whole concept of denial and judgments of life's experiences was the root cause for disease and its widespread control over human life in the past.

He could remember being consumed with the need to find happiness and love even while he had been living it amply. It had been the driving force through Niti's life and all she had done was simply lived. But that had obviously raised her energies to the point that two lifetimes later here he was – one of the most advanced souls on earth.

Going back into a deep sheetla mode immediately, he called out clearly and sharply for soul energies that he sought, to come into his vibrational zone.

Nothing. Neither a movement nor a sense of connection developed. There was nothing in his conscious vicinity.

Skolt sat distractedly while his junior researchers' team discussed and debated issues around him. Physical sound-wise there was absolute silence in the garden where they had assembled for this discussion, but in his head ... ! Wow! They were making such a racket! He wanted to switch them off but he was supposed to be moderating this discussion ...

It almost felt like the Niti lifetime again. He had Salil on his mind all the time. He couldn't seem to do anything without returning to this thought at the completion of work at hand. He was reliving the past.

It obviously meant that compulsions were going to be the way of the soul as long as you were in human form. It mattered not how high your energy rose, the soul was still going to direct you towards more and more. So what was this? Was he supposed to overcome this again, like in the last lifetime or was he to attain this union like he had craved in the last lifetime. What?

Skolt excused himself and switched the others off. He contemplated deeply with his soul and his higher energies. Help me figure this out and we'll close this chapter, he said. That soul energy seems to be important to me, said the soul. You can search the Akashic Records, said the higher energies, but we doubt you'll be able to access personal records of another.

Yes, that was the way of the Akashic Records. Almost like a personal password that 'Internet' and 'cloud' had required in the past, one's energies were the natural password to access all information past and present that related with that energy and was stored in the Records. Deep contemplation of any other generic concept also led to that area of knowledge opening up to ones energies. Of course, one travelled within and one imbibed only as much as one's energies corresponded to. Personal information though, remained shrouded and there was no way or means to access that without the energy code. If an individual opened their life to you, you could walk into their energy and view their entire history but until then . . . There was no way of knowing another's journey.

He could go back to Niti's lifetime, and with his advanced soul energies, he was able to see civilisation and people as they lived and created history. It was like watching a movie. Public figures, famous people and events were available for detailed viewing because they always carried geographic and evolutionary knowledge in them. Individual lives, though, one could never trace. Even though he knew the year and the geographic area of occurrence, unless Salil had become famous or come under the public glare or done something monumental, he would not feature in Skolt's energy field.

And yet Skolt scanned the Records for that time period, going back and forth through those years. Who knows when Salil had left his body? Or maybe he had invented something in his lifetime! As a marketing professional? Highly unlikely, he mocked himself. Keeping the inner dialogue going, Skolt went through the years 1969–2040 a number of times, hoping he'd pick up a clue.

Nothing.

Skolt released his consciousness from the grip of the past and decided to focus on something else.

Unknown to Skolt, though, his roughing through memory lane of those years of ADY were bringing it into focus for others who had a connection with that time but had not bothered to be aware of it so far.

As always, nothing the universe addresses ever goes waste. Neither did Skolt's efforts!

What better way to distract himself than the young team's debates, thought Skolt, tapping into their discussion again and trying to read where it was going.

Julio – a young, quiet, meticulous member, added to the group for his love of numbers – seemed especially animated today.

'Skolt!' Julio exclaimed, the minute he noticed Skolt had signed in, 'You won't believe what I just saw!'

Yes, Julio was excited. Skolt couldn't seem to drum up enough emotion but he responded anyway.

'What?' Skolt asked uninterestedly.

'All this talk about past civilisations seems to have awakened my access to the Records too! I can remember a lifetime in the ADY when I was a youth reformer in India. And yes, all the understanding of religion and limitations and lack of understanding just makes so much of sense now. I can see how we were ignorant of so many facts then and how that led to the muddle of existence we created. I was a Muslim youth then.' Julio kept up his story without a break.

'"Muslim" was related to another religion in those days called Islam. I was a young man named Salil, fighting for unity and accep—'

Julio gasped as if in pain. 'Skolt! What are you doing?'

Skolt stopped immediately. He was roughing through Julio's energy without even realising it! He had pushed his energy into Julio with such force it was equivalent to physically pushing him up against a wall and breathing down his face!

'Sorry. What did you say again?'

Julio seemed to have gone into his shell again immediately. 'What? What did I say?' he asked meekly. There was no fear. Nobody had any fear in this era. They could sense the other's aura and everyone knew that the other meant no harm. There was no need for harm and pain and hurt. But yes, tactics like rough-shodding another could still shock! Idiot! Skolt berated himself and calming his energies repeated, 'You said you were a young boy called Salil? And . . . ?'

'And . . . well . . . it was a short life. I got into youth protests and activism in war torn countries. I remember being sick, like I had contracted some dreadful disease and I believe I died at an early age.' Julio stopped. 'That's it. Nothing more.'

'Sit in sheetla and contemplate it. A lot more will come from there. You will know your lifetimes after that and how those actions framed your journey to where you are today. Study the pattern.' Skolt kept his voice calm.

False alarm.

The morning continued with discussions of varying intensity but Skolt chose not to focus. After a respectable period, he excused himself and physically moved towards his community room.

'What made you so edgy, Skolt?' He felt Julio's question just before he could close his aura. He opened it again.

'Edgy?'

'Was it mentioning the time period or something else?' he could sense Julio's curiosity.

'Your name.' Skolt admitted sincerely. 'Salil. It has special significance for me.'

'Salil? From that time period?'

'Yes. It was too much of a coincidence, right? The universe has always had a perverse sense of humour.' Skolt shook his head self-mockingly.

'Well, Anita had a lifetime with the same name. I can ask her when.' Julio continued thoughtfully.

'Anita?'

'In fact, why don't we make that another kind of research?' now he sounded excited! 'Let's ask people to search their past lives and give us their past-life names! We can create all kinds of data with that. We might even find a pattern for . . .' Julio drifted off, sensing Skolt's sceptic exasperation.

'Anita?' Skolt repeated quietly. False alarm again? He didn't want to indulge his fantasies.

'Yes. Well, she's a friend. She's an artist and she's just started with carving the caves down at the rocky bay on the left coast. The new project? That's her baby.'

'Just started? As in – the last three weeks maybe?' Skolt tried to sound nonchalant. He just hoped he'd succeeded!

'Exactly three weeks, actually!' Julio looked at Skolt in amazement. Nothing Skolt did or knew surprised his team anymore. They thought he was omnipresent anyway! But Julio, this time, looked surprised.

'Will you tell her I'd like to meet her sometime? And also find out about her Salil lifetime timeline. If it fits – I definitely want to meet her.'

Julio nodded.

'Thanks.' Skolt added as an afterthought.

Chapter 6

He was curious. He had never been curious. At least not in the last two lifetimes that he could remember. But he was curious now.

What did his soul energy want? Was it taking him towards a challenge or towards gratification? Whatever the reason may be, he had managed to create a thrill of excitement in his life. He was looking forward to the unknown. Too much was always known to him . . .

Two days later, Skolt couldn't wait for Julio to get back to him anymore. He was suddenly impatient today. He decided to walk down to the caves. He'd just take a look around, he thought.

And so, later that day Skolt made his way to the waterside on the left coast. It was a beautiful day and the sea gulls flew past creating white streaks in the sky. Skolt took the time to stop and take in the scenery and the feeling and the sense of peace and balance the world created within him. He usually preferred the trees and forests and green life for balance and to synchronise his energies. He was an earth and ether energy. Water and sand he visited less. It felt good today though. The sounds were soothing.

Skolt walked onto the project site and immediately did the soothing effects of water leave him. He could feel the buzzing of his energy! No false alarm this. There was something to be had here. He could feel his heart plexus squeeze and vibrations burst out of him, some coming back immediately to hit him hard in the chest. This then was excitement, he supposed, with that part of his mind that was still dispassionate.

He walked around the site calmly, as though his heart wasn't thudding hard enough to burst! But he wasn't fooling anyone. His energy was obviously too intense to contain and people around either got out of his way or stared from a distance. The commotion was enough to distract the most dedicated and focused worker too. Skolt walked around blithely, pretending like he didn't know what he was doing.

Nothing. Not again! False alarm? No, he'd felt the buzz. Skolt decided to walk back past the project site again, and if he didn't see an energy equal he'd just go sit by the water and cool off maybe.

Skolt continued his walk with considerable less energy and drama than the first time around. Walking slowly past the carvings, he noticed how beautifully they were coming along. Details were painstakingly made into facial expressions and forms of humans and animals and nature. He couldn't help but admire the craftsmanship.

And then he felt it – The zing of a questioning energy tapping his aura. The energy was coming from a nearby source. He looked around to find the source. And there it was. The same energy. The very same intense, dark eyes.

Only now those eyes belonged to a lovely, petite, young – really young – girl! And they were looking at him hesitantly, and questioningly.

Skolt felt his excitement rise immediately. The thudding, buzzing, whizzing – all happening at once! He consciously calmed his energies and opened his aura to her.

'Do I know you?' she questioned.

'Why do you ask?'

'You seem familiar, but I can't place you.' He could sense she was scanning his energy and trying very hard to place him.

'Yes. I believe we did know each other. A very long time ago, maybe.'

'Really?' she tried harder to remember. 'Sorry. I just can't seem to remember.' She did sound sorry.

'It probably wasn't a memorable enough association?' Skolt sounded like he was making a casual comment while all he wanted was to walk up to her and look into her eyes till she recognised him. Not memorable? The memory hadn't left him in 12,000 years! And he hadn't been memorable?

'No. I'm sure I would remember you. Your energies are too strong.' Yes! Right answer! She was interested. Something was obviously nudging her.

'They didn't used to be this strong when we met last. It's possible you can't relate.'

'When was that?'

For the first time in his life, Skolt wanted to bridge the physical gap between him and another. He wanted to actually, physically, be with her when he reminded her.

Walking up to her as casually as he could manage, Skolt said, 'When you were Salil.'

Her energies froze. He could sense that clearly. She clamped down on him. 'What?'

He didn't reply. She would figure it out. If his love and his cries for union had had any power at all, she would remember.

'How do you know . . . ? My "Salil" lifetime?!' Incredulous. He could feel it coming off her in waves.

She looked at him intently from the distance separating them and he could feel her scanning his energies like needles tearing him apart. She was still very young. She wouldn't be able to penetrate his aura enough to connect to his Akashic

Records. The best of them couldn't do it and she was still new to him. He knew it would stump her.

But she simply switched off her energies and turned back to her calm. Just like that. She gave up on making a connection – just like that.

'Anita?'

No response.

'May I talk to you?'

No response.

'I could help you remember.'

Absolutely no response.

She probably had a steely will. An inner strength that came from tempering one's will rather than learning from reactions.

That's right! Make it a repeat of circumstances. The stony silences, the desperate need for communication, the trying and waiting in endless circles. Yeah, yeah, yeah . . . he knew how this was going to end.

Wait a minute. Desperate need . . . ? What was he – in the twenty-first century again? How did one get desperate, and needy(!), in this era?

He stood in the cave a while longer and sent out his energy. He couldn't read her at all. And that was really, really surprising. He found it almost effortless to read lesser energy souls. That was his life's work, after all.

But life, the cunning thing, had more work in store for him. There was finally something in his life that he could not achieve effortlessly. He almost laughed out loud. This should be fun.

No, he meant that seriously. He wasn't being sarcastic. He could feel the buzz of excitement. This *was* going to be fun! Anita may never speak to him and his wishes and desires may remain unfulfilled, but he knew that the higher energies were not done with him yet. There were still things on this earth he had not experienced yet. No need to be complacent and Mr-Know-It-All, he mocked himself. Time to be a learner and student again!

He strode out of the caves and onto the sandy beach in a much different state of mind than he had been when he got there. He had heart plexus areas to explore and learn. And he was ready. Bring it on ye source of all things disruptive! He murmured. His cat-and-mouse game with the universe was back on!

Anita sensed the burning gaze and energy fading away and she slowly turned to look at the spot where the man had been standing. He was gone. Who was he? Why did he feel like this?

'Every successive generation in the ascending cycle is obviously more intelligent and slightly more wise than the previous, right?' Danube paused for breath, 'and every generation in the descending cycle is losing a little bit of their wisdom.' Pause again, but more was obviously coming.

'And we are in the descending cycle. So we are less intelligent than the seniors and our children will be that little bit lesser than us. Not a nice thought,'

No. Not a nice thought at all. But Skolt was distracted and not in the pacifier mode.

'It takes thousands of years for the change to occur.' Leave it to Isabella to play the pacifier; she always came through.

'But that's how the energy is flowing, right? Downwards.'

'Yes, so what's your point Danube?' Elina sounded impatient.

'Which means that the books and documents we put out in this era will be the deepest and closest to truth interpretations that will ever be made for the next 15,000 years at least!'

That got Skolt's attention.

'Yes, Danube. You're right about that. That is why, as one of the first generations of the descending cycle, we need to record the facts in forms that can be accessed and understood for the next complete cycle. And we need to do it now. You can understand my urgency now, can't you?'

'And every descending Satya Yuga does it? They just know to do it?'

'Yes. There are always advanced souls in a yuga that are higher than average energy and they understand the need. In fact, I was just thinking about it the other day. How scripts like the Upanishads and Yoga Sutras survived and guided mankind through the knowledge gathering eras of AKY and ADY. And how prevalent understandings of the Satya Yuga like the Mayan civilisations and the Greek and Egyptian lifestyles influenced people's thinking enough to create curiosity and stories to help understand facts that they couldn't comprehend in the Kalyuga.'

'Stories?'

'Well, yes. All the mythological stories that lived for centuries were people's attempts to explain the facts that they knew should be true but they just could not understand. So mythological characters with special powers and ugly desires were created to explain the abilities of the ancient humans!' Skolt smiled as he remembered some of the stories he had heard in his previous lifetimes. And the one prior to Niti's! Oh my! The superstitions they had then!

'So they blindly believed something they thought should be true but they didn't really sense? Without experiencing it?'

'Yes, Elina. And you should sound surprised too! Humans became superstitious and fearful and that led them further into a dark and scary life because they actually believed things they could not prove. And that meant that they imagined even more that weren't existent. And that can be a scary place – mankind's imagination.'

'And that's probably where the belief in God and faith in Him came in.'

'Yes. Their belief that there is someone, somewhere who loves them enough to deliver them from all their fears. Who will magically make it all OK. God.'

'But we are aware of The Source and not *someone,* but surely we believe that the energy of The Source will always guide us. Isn't that the same thing?'

'Is it? Yes, that was a physically real lifetime and they had to convert The Source energy into form and structure before they could create a connection with it. So they had God and they had icons and deities and symbols and they gave them names and lives and entire stories to make them real, so they could develop faith. Today we live in an energy world and we connect with The Source as energy. In so far, it is the same. But do we believe that The Source controls, directs and creates our lives' individually? Do we need to defend It's sanctity or protect It's office from slander and abuse? Do we have various paths and processes to achieve union with It? Do we even believe that we need to achieve union with It?'

He could feel most of the team in sheetla, trying to create understanding of those ancient beliefs when human beings felt incomplete and inadequate as themselves. When they struggled for union, either with other human beings or with nature or with their God to feel complete. It must have been a hard, hard time. Because they knew now that if one could not find one's completeness in oneself, that is – to know your soul and your strong and weak areas and pick your area of effort – one would never create union with anyone or anything. One would always be incomplete which would further result in fruitless unions leading to dissatisfaction and frustrations. And these emotions would take one further away from reading one's soul. A vicious and pointless cycle.

'OK, so we have scriptures that most can't understand, which leads to mythological tales, which leads to fear and faith in God or Gods, which leads to frustrating and pointless efforts to attain Him.' That was Elina's organised mind categorising the theory.

'Yes. Which naturally leads to acceptance of the fact that there is more to living than fear and superstitions and a God, I guess.' Skolt was distracted again. He was feeling a delicate energy nudge.

'Which will have the wise looking for answers and they will discover the ancient scriptures again. Aha!'

'But who is to say they will interpret the scriptures rightly this time, Skolt? They're still not at the energy level of those that wrote the scriptures.'

'They don't need to be. They need to interpret it for their people in that time period. As long as the direction is right, the scriptures can be interpreted a million different ways. People only have to be accepting of new interpretations as they are discovered to be able to smoothly transcend the yuga changes. That rarely happens!'

The feeling died down. Skolt knew what it was. It was Anita trying to find him. She hadn't received his response. She had closed her energies before he could place or return her nudge. He could send out to her, but he decided to wait. She would try again. Maybe.

'So the wise will just sit down one day and figure out the Akashic Records?'

'No. Ummm . . . yes, in a way.'

Every one of them was in deep sheetla, following his train of thought perfectly.

'In the ascending cycle just gone by there are many who accessed the Akashic Records but were not aware of it. The famous scientist Einstein actually claimed to find answers to his biggest invention blocks in his sleep! He had almost 500 patents to his name, if you please. He was not aware of it, but his deep contemplation of an issue or a problem actually created enough energy for him to access that area of the Akashic Records and the answers came to him. Almost all scientists at that time were intense, high energy souls. Whether they found solutions while taking a bath or sitting under a tree or even when physically incapacitated. The final breakthrough always occurred when deep contemplation led to access to the Records. Because they were not aware of their soul energy or the Records, the answers came during the calm after the contemplation when the accessed information floated into their mind energy and it felt almost like a eureka moment! So yes, the wise will access the Records, but no, they will not sit down and do so consciously.'

'These were scientists proving physical realities. What about the subtler energies?'

'At the onset of Kalyuga, many prophets interpreted the scriptures in simple, easy forms to help mankind get through the period they knew was going to be difficult. The 2,400 years of darkness. There was Krishna and Buddha and Jesus Christ. Their teachings became the very scriptures that led mankind through, and out of, the Dark Ages. Even through the Kalyuga, many more prophets came. They came with higher soul energy to reinforce the direction steadily upwards and onwards. As Kalyuga started to move out, prophets gave way to poets and gurus and masters and guides. No more was religion the guiding force. But towards the end of the ADY even those had become few and far away. Humans had understood their power and they were happy to use it.'

'So they can now access the records?'

'No, but they can begin to understand the scriptures, on their own, without commentary. A wise sage called Adi Shankaracharya, who lived in the Indian subcontinent in the era of DKY, had said it first. As Adi Shankaracharya explained earlier in 8 CE, knowledge of the texts can only come from *nididhyāsana*, prolonged study of and contemplation on the truths revealed in the texts and contemplation of non-duality.

Nididhyasana leads to *anubhav*, direct cognition or understanding, which establishes the truth of the studies. Adi Shankaracharya holds *anubhava* to be a *pramana*, an independent source of knowledge, which is provided by *nididhyasana*.

'Two interpreters, Davis and Hirst, later tried to simplify it. Davis translates *anubhava* as "direct intuitive understanding". According to Hirst, *anubhava* is the 'non-dual realisation gained from the scriptures', which 'provides the sanction and paradigm for proper reasoning'.

'Basically this means long and deep sheetla on each part of the text till it reveals its truth intuitively.'

The team stayed in the sheetla mode even after Skolt stopped transmitting his reply. He could sense they were rummaging through history and trying to create a storyline through the ages.

He decided to leave them to it.

'Skolt?'
'Skolt!'
One was Hoyt and the other . . . ? Anita? . . . Yes! Anita!
'Give me a little time, Hoyt.'
'Anita?'
'Yes . . .'
'You found out my name.'

Silence.

'Did you find out anything else?' Why was she so hesitant, he wondered. There was nothing to fear. There were no misunderstandings or compulsions in today's day. He could understand when people relied on words and body language that misinterpretations and cross-purposes did occur. But today? Today people only read each other's energies and energies could never be misunderstood. They were clear and real and always the truth.

'My Salil lifetime? I can't seem to access it. Never have. I only know I died of heart trouble.'

The heart, eh? And she doesn't know why.

Skolt almost smiled as he thought of the twists and turns that life created and where they led to.

The heart plexus it was – an impossible theory in those days but so obvious and understandable today.

Oh! The amount of time man had wasted doing what his intellect told him to ... Eras ... !

'That could be a reason you've blocked out that life. The heart.'

'Huh?'

'The heart trouble would mean a deep heart plexus block, even if they didn't call it that in those days. Maybe you'd closed your heart plexus so tight that today you can't access that life. Access is only through the heart plexus, after all.'

'And where do you come into the picture?'

'If you don't remember me, I must not have been important.'

'But you remember me.'

'Oh, I remember a lot of things! Some completely irrelevant stuff too!' He tried making light of it, though the Niti in him could feel the knife twisting again. That forgettable, was I?

'Yes, you do have very strong energies.'

'You do too.'

'I do?'

'Not many people can block me out. But you managed quite effortlessly the last time.'

He sensed her smile and the slight easing of her uncomfortableness.

'I'm not really interested in remembering either, frankly. No point.'

No! Really? She wasn't even a little curious?

'If that was the only reason for your making connection, I'm sorry. I can't help you with that.' Her energies were mellifluous. Delicate and gentle, just like her eyes. Like her energies of before.

He was silent for a while. And then he thought, 'Why not? Let's just go for it . . .'

'Actually you *can* help me. I have some unfinished business from that lifetime and it relates to you, Anita, or to Salil, that is. I need to connect with your energies now, just to clear that block that seems to have travelled centuries with me. Maybe it would clear your blocks too. We can try?'

Lame, Skolt. So lame.

'I'm in a relationship.'

Chapter closed. Cycle of life, history repeats, blah, blah, blah . . . damn it!

'So?' he snapped.

Silence.

'I'm not asking for a relationship. No sukhsa or tulsna involved. Gosh, you're a kid yet. I just need to get to know you better. Walk through your energies and close certain chapters of my life.'

'No. I don't want you to.'

'I can't do this on my own. Please?' And that was a huge thing for Skolt to say. There was nothing, or close to nothing that he could not do in his human form.

'I'm sorry.'

He felt her recede. Slowly. Like she felt bad doing this to him. Then why was she? He hadn't asked for anything impossible. Every soul helped every other soul today. Why was she not?

He let her go. It was her journey and there was nothing more he could say.

He hoped the niggling sensation would leave him now. He hoped he was free of the Niti lifetime. His soul had to accept that there was nothing he could do. Yet again.

'Skolt? Are you available?'

'Yes, Hoyt.'

'You OK, Skolt?'

'Yes.'

'I can barely hear you. The energy is so faint. You're not projecting well.' It took a lot to disturb Hoyt, but obviously not being able to receive Skolt's signals clearly could.

'I'm OK. Where are we with the book?'

'Yes,' and that's all it took to return Hoyt's focus back to the work at hand, 'even though your connecting intelligence to the evolution of the soul is what got us to give shape and structure to this document, we've decide to leave evolution of the soul for another time. We can do the next document on that. For now we've simplified the yugas and their connection with the gradual rise and fall of intelligence and left it at that. Would you like to go through that?'

'Convert it into readable sheets and leave them in my file please? I'll go through it in detail later.'

'Are you seriously OK, Skolt?' Kiera's query wafted in.

'Yes.' He replied, more gently. He knew the others must be wondering the same thing – They had just completed their assignment and Skolt wasn't all eager and excited like he usually was. Strange behaviour for Skolt.

He switched off his energies almost immediately and walked into the forest for some balance and deep sheetla.

Was this really going to be a repeat of that earlier lifetime? Was he going to use her refusal to be with him as reason to build up this great big sense of rejection and lost love and wallow in it forever?

No, that wasn't fair. This wasn't a rejection and it didn't feel like it. But that had been and that's exactly what it had felt like. No need to belittle his emotions just so he could deal with them.

So, what were the facts here?

That Niti had been so insignificant in Salil's life that he couldn't even remember her, while he had been the raison d'etre of hers. Did the universe work like that? So much discrepancy? He didn't think so.

What didn't add up? Why would he be so restless for something that didn't exist.

Not in a physical reality, no, it didn't exist. But there were other realities that existed and they had certain compulsions of their own. And unfinished business in any reality was still unfinished business. The perfectionist stickler of a soul would not settle for anything less than neatly tied up ends.

Even if that only meant acceptance of the heart plexus for the consequences, whether they be happy or sad. And his heart plexus was not ready to accept. It still angled for answers. Well, he had tried answers. It wasn't happening.

Skolt sat in sheetla for a long, long time, going through numerous lifetimes to see in how many he and Anita had connected and what had been the pattern.

But he didn't discover anything new. They had always been soulmates with intense love and hate relationships through lifetimes. Ambivalent mediocrity was not for them. She didn't want to acknowledge him and the soul refused to recognise his for the last two lifetimes, well, so be it.

He was cured. He was going to leave this journey with that one soul connection incomplete and he was perfectly OK with it.

Skolt walked into his room later that day, refreshed and ready to go through the finished 'Book of Intelligence'.

Intelligence is circular.
12,000 years rising and another 12,000 declining.

The latest cycle:
Scriptures of spiritual importance and energy living were written as far back as DSY. The old Indian scriptures give information on stars and constellations and space to the last, fine detail. Astronomy and astrology is thousands of years old according to these books and yet the telescope was invented only in AD 600. Greek Mythology also mentions stars and planets and other information that we later claimed in ADY, was discovered only in the last 1,000 years, since the telescope. Yet, men have known it from long before.

Knowledge of naturally healing technology and aerodynamics were seen till DTY.

And of interest is the fact that we have excavated sites like, Mohen-jo-daro and Harrappa that talk of advanced civilisations that existed from 3300 BC – 1700 BC. (DDY) with pre-Harappan cultures starting c. 7500 BCE. (DTY) The Indus Valley civilisation, the Egyptian civilisation, the Mayan civilisations are all examples of highly evolved intelligence. They had knowledge of metallurgy, of textile, of town planning complete with sewage and water drainage! The Egyptian Civilisation had such phenomenal knowledge of construction that their pyramids and structures stand tall and proud even till ADY when those modern-day constructions were falling apart in the face of earthquakes and floods and other natural disasters

All these advanced ways of life and living and then nothing. A darkness came upon existence. When the wise struggled to create hope and faith in the hearts of mankind to keep them going.

Religion and God were discovered. That quickly turned back upon itself and in a few centuries this very faith and belief was used to oppress and suppress the souls. Power, greed, and domination reared its ugly head. And it stayed for the longest time. At least till the yuga changed.

Proof of descent into less than 20 per cent intelligence bracket.

The darkness gave way to discoveries – electricity, magnetism, atomic energy, gravity, the printing press, the steam engine and many, many more.

Peace and love and support for all of humanity and nature started to enter man's consciousness. Harmony was attempted. Love was a founding corner stone to relationships.

From 4250 ATY, souls started to show distinct signs of harmony and comprehension of magnetic energy began. Crystal healing, magnetic healing, balanced living, natural fuels, spiritual energy and many other forms of health and living flourished for the next 3,000 years.

The rise of intelligence was completed in the next 4,000 years when man accomplished complete energy synchronisation with the higher energies and his own soul energies.

Skolt thought how this book resembled the writings of thousands of years ago – cryptic, non-explanatory, and terse.

Perfect.

It left enough scope for interpretation and research.

The yuga theory:

The relevance study:

Skolt lay on his bed. He thought he'd close his eyes for a while. He wasn't fit to go out anyway. His energies were too involved with his internal self.

And she walked in.

She physically walked into his energy space. Into his very room!

No gentle nudge or a signal or a polite request to connect. No! Right here in front of him. And he hadn't had a clue.

Still very young, was she? Lesser energy? Really?

No sukhsa or tulsna was he interested in. Yeah. Right.

His heart plexus was beating like an old African drum and his kundalini plexus just had to calm down or he would never again be able to convince himself that he was a wise soul on extended vacation on this earth.

And what was she doing here anyway?

Skolt sat up slowly.

He still wasn't sure what was happening here.

'It's become a habit to block you out', she started softly.

'Huh?'

'I've done it for so long that now I do it almost unconsciously.'

'You've accessed the . . .'

'Yes.'

They looked at each other for a long time. Their energies were silent too.

'Why didn't you ever come back?'

She shook her head.

'Sure!'

Idiot. You sound like an old-fashioned fool. Sharp up!

'You said you wanted connection. I'm willing to try.'

And just like that she turned around and walked out his door. Just like that! Again.

By the time Skolt gathered his wits around him and followed her, she was gone, and he couldn't sense her anywhere close by either.

'Why didn't you ever come back?' he repeated into her energy space anyway.

She was very, very good at containing her energies . . . Or else . . . there was something else going on here that he wasn't getting a grip on.

They would try and connect, and he would figure it out. After all, he was from a generation of close to 100 per cent brain potential, wasn't he?

Sure, hotshot! We'll look forward to that one . . .

. . . To be continued with *The Evolution of the Soul*

Bibliography

Adi Shankaracharya – Stotras
Sri Sri Swami Sri Yukteswar Giri – The Holy Science
The laws of Manu – Penguin classics
Developing a Universal religion – Wikibooks
The Upanishads – Eknath Easwaran
On the Origin of Species – Charles Darwin

Influences:
Science papers on Evolution of Religion
Religious books of all religions.
Shri Shri Paramahansa Yogananda's teachings
Upanishads by Adi Shankaracharya

Printed in the United States
By Bookmasters